The Pentrich & South Wingfield Revolution Group was formed
initially to celebrate the bi-centenary of the 1817 Pentrich
Revolution. This is a largely forgotten struggle, which was an
important step in our history. Books have been written about the
main perpetrators but very little is known about the women
involved. Although this is a fictional account, it is based on fact
and could be regarded as a love story.

The P.S.W.R.G. are committed to keeping the memory of the 1817
Pentrich Revolution alive and continue to bring it to the wider
public.

As this book is not a 'heavy historical tome,' it is a welcome
addition to our library.

Valerie Herbert
Secretary/Trustee
PSWRG
2019

Cover design by Thomas Oliver Matthews-Bee

CONTENTS

2

PREFACE

A tale of love and heroism comes down the years, after the industrial revolution tore the lives of so many apart. The government's response was one repressive dictate after another.

The story aims to give a more humane side to those slandered by the history books and show how the establishment in the most questionable way possible, blocked the rights we now take for granted.

History appears to tarnish those who stepped beyond the boundary to fight injustice. Many far closer to heroic than those we supposedly admire.

I wanted to portray Jeremiah and those who marched with him, the way I see them, men who fought to free their families and those they saw suffering from a life of abject poverty.

Having always been aware of the story, it appeared to have been pushed away like an old book within a Library, so inspired by my family's love of history and meeting members of the Pentrich and South Wingfield Revolution Group who keep that memory alive, I decided to write the story the way I see it.

My thanks go to the Pentrich and South Wingfield Revolution Group, for the help I have received, also the volunteers at the Ruddington, Framework Knitters Museum and Sutton Living Memory. With special thanks to Patrick Cook, Valerie Herbet, and Sylvia Mason. A. M. Matthews.

Jeremiah Brandreth

As he appeared on his Trial for High Treason at the Special

Assizes held in Derby Oct 16th 1817

Reproduced with the kind Permission of Derby Local Studies and Family History

Library

The years are long and apt to hide all memory, as one by one those who remembered all are called away. On occasion memories may reappear and time reveals its hidden treasure. Those with courage come forth again, along with those without and if you care to look you may find them waiting there.

The vilified may have the bravest heart.

The

Ninth

Of

June

A. M. Matthews

Chapter One

WALKING OUT

Ann Bridget had seen this young man many times before having arrived in town earlier in the year. Now he sat outside The New Inn on the Green talking as always. Whispers were he was involved with the Luddite gangs, breaking the frames that produced shoddy goods, allowing the Shiners to earn a proper wage again.

"What if I went over Sal?" Already in a state of self-induced panic just proposing it.

"You won't." Safe in the knowledge Ann wasn't about to lower herself and true to form she was having second thoughts.

"You ever seen him with anyone Sal?" Forcing the handle to get the water gushing into the pail from the pump that stood proudly on the Green. Having no running water at Bedlam Court, it was a constant battle to keep up with what was needed.

Sal couldn't get her words out before Ann turned to find him watching. Looking back in wide-eyed excitement, not wanting to breathe for fear she shattered this small joy. In a sudden rush the water overflowed the pail soaking the bottom of her dress, the excuse she'd needed that allowed her near enough to be noticed. Quickly lifting the dress without going too far in case the lads were privy to more than she wanted. Wringing it out along with the crisp white underskirt, which was quite a fine thing having been given by her Aunt on her birthday. All picked because her mother said fawn showed off the colour of her hair, that was held under a crisp white bonnet tied in a bow under her chin.

The area around the pump often stood in mud, so the girls would tiptoe across to the huge flagstone that stood before it. Then go carefully back to avoid the consequences of not doing so, this being difficult holding a pail full of water. Ann adjusted the bonnet, it having slipped to one side, feeling slightly foolish. On occasion a lad would come to lift the pail over the mud for them, then the girls would take it one each side of the handle to its destination.

Sal made a stifled little cough.

"You'll need help, by the looks of it." A hand reached forward to hoist up the pail before Ann could speak. The young man with the warm brown eyes stood in front of her, the water overflowing the pail akin to a pendulum swinging from one side to the other.

Forgetting her manners, she'd just enough forethought to smile back. Staring into the most tranquil of expressions, yet those warm brown eyes left Ann wondering if he could read every thought she had.

"We goin' this way?" Bringing her back into the present while gesturing in the direction Ann was looking.

"Ahm,' yes up the steps," following like she'd been struck by the hand of the almighty, she cast an amazed glance in Sal's direction.

Reaching the steps, he turned, looking at the bottom of the dress before going up to Crier's yard, "be best if you go first, or

—

you'll get another drenching," his face more serious than before.

Swallowing Ann gave an embarrassed smile, trying to think of something bright to say, but right at the moment she would've settled for anything.

Holding the pail as if it were of no weight, her gallant helper moved to the side with the utmost courtesy. Ann hurried up the narrow steps, past Crier's yard, then up to Bedlam Court.

The streets, like most in the area were pushed together in a jumble of dark squares, appearing to hem each other in, with little room from one side of the street to the other. A narrow road running between the houses with enough room for a cart and a bit more; on dry days lines of washing hung from the upstairs windows from one side to the other hoping to catch the breeze.

Ann rapped upon the door not wanting to go in and squander the only connection she'd ever had with this young man. Praying one of her sisters answered, while the bottom of the dress clung uncomfortably about her ankles.

Glancing upwards, olive skin and dark curling hair framed the warm brown eyes and now she saw that expression again. There was something in it that melted every bit of reserve Ann tried to muster. Rapping upon the door a second time, which left the impression it was too small for the house, although it was like all the rest. This time it opened instantly, George Bridget stood in front of them without a word.

Ann's helper gave a broad smile. "Your daughter needed some assistance." Placing the pail onto the doorstep.

<hr>

There was a delayed sniff. "Did she?" Eyeing his daughter skeptically, "thank yu' lad. I'll put it with t'others then." A hand engrained with the dust of his work that would never wash away shoved the pail just inside the doorway. Turning back to them, glancing in the direction of Ann's helper "behave tha' sen," who didn't appear put out any, while Ann discovered a richer shade of red.

George Bridget examined his daughter. "You with Sally Marshall?"

"Sal's on the Green waiting for me. You don't need me, do you?" Praying he didn't say.

"No thank yu' lass. I think we can manage. Dun't be late in. Your mother will be whittlin'." With another glance toward his daughter's new acquaintance, George Bridget picked up the pail and shut the door.

Leaving Ann to wonder what he'd say when she got home, then remembering her manners. "Thank you, it's really kind of you to bring it all the way up here."

"Thought you'd be wet through if I didn't; I'm Jeremiah by the way. I was wonderin' if you'd join us."

"Ann, Ann Bridget." The smile that lit her face at such an invitation disappeared almost instantly. "I don't think my father would approve." Thinking how many lads were on the Green, trying to swallow her disappointment. They walked together past Crier's yard, down the steps, only to hear the group upon the Green getting more and more boisterous.

A few sat by the River Idle, throwing a cloth about they'd filched off the barmaid, the river being more like a stream, swelling sometimes making the lane off it extremely muddy. While the Green served as a meeting place for the town, with the Maypole to one side, Tenter Lane running in the same direction as the Idle, until the little river turned towards the dam.

Most of the lads were still outside The New Inn, which looked lovely in its fresh paint, being a bit more of a job than was first realised. Joe Markham the village clown was inclined to give the steps a shove every time the man reached the top of the ladder. Still the inn looked stunning against the lovely stone for which the town was well known. Everyone proud it was used on some quite prestigious buildings throughout the country, taken from the quarry next to Smedley's End.

A brown-haired young man who usually sat with Jeremiah settled next to Sal, who stood waiting there without a care.

Jeremiah walked towards them, "This is Bill, looks like you've met already." He smiled.

Both girls trilled a greeting like they'd rehearsed it, to be met by an embarrassed grunt. Bill was taller than Jeremiah, with a mass of brown wavy hair that seemed to match his character.

Sal looked him up and down half smiling. "Saw you the other day, doing the juggling." Always more direct than anyone anticipated because she looked so innocent. In truth Ann was inclined to hide behind Sal's confidence when they were together.

"Hope you enjoyed it? I were good, weren't I?" Awaiting a

confirmation that didn't come.

Giving no reply Sal took off the little bonnet she was wearing to let a cascade of blonde curls fall about her shoulders, "Don't know that good describes it." Eyes shining with the same delicious mischief that lay there moments ago, replacing the bonnet and turning away smiling broadly.

"Here Bill tha' might need this." A soaking wet cloth landed with a thud in the middle of Bill's shoulders, Joe Markham's brother, Rueben not far behind his sibling in his behaviour.

Ann stood trying not to laugh.

While Bill picked up the towel and threw it back into the inn, mouthing a few choice words at Rueben he wasn't going to utter now.

Jeremiah ignored them. "What if the four of us took a walk over to the dam?"

Ann and Sal considered this a good idea, while Jeremiah took the ale from Bill he'd nursed till was warm, finishing most, then stepping through the inn doorway, to place it on the long worn table just inside, turning back to them. "Anyhow I've four sisters, so fetchin' water's something I know about. It's why I left."

Ann gave an unimpressed exaggerated sigh, while Jeremiah wiped his mouth on the back of his hand, to erase the grin he wore. "Saw you when t' Romani's were here; when Bill did his juggling."

Truth was Ann always watched this young man with a stealth many would be proud of. "You ne…" Stopping before going any further.

At least Jeremiah's Luddite days gave him the edge on some things, knowing instantly if someone took more interest in what he was doing than was normal.

Ann considered the remark a compliment, even if it wasn't true.

"I've been trying to look clever to impress you."

Raising her eyebrows trying not to laugh. "Really." Starting to feel more confident. "Well, let us all know when you can."

Grinning at her while walking backwards a few paces, he turned in the direction of the dam, the girls hurriedly took each other's arm to follow on up the incline, while Bill sprinted to catch up with Jeremiah.

Up past the farm and the blacksmith's yard, through the little rickety fence towards Unwin's dam. Talking of their work and when the Romani's had been, who always put on a show, while the lads lost money on the tricks they came out with. The dancing and fiddle playing a source of entertainment that went on well into the night.

Settling by the trees next to the Idle, the little river tumbling toward the dam, which kept them from the eyes of those who lived there. If the owner's came past, however, they generally shared the time of day with anyone inclined to be there, unlike some. Always riding by in a phaeton carriage, studded with brass nails, with four huge wheels, both horses having bob tails, while the coachman's hair had a life all of its own. It was a fine sight, and the whole town knew instantly who it was, for the mill employed many in the town. A great deal of the work being stored inside the fine house in which the Unwin's resided, which amused some of their guests.

They sat upon the grass watching the little river scurry toward the water wheel that turned steadily hour on hour. Bill and Jeremiah regressing into their childhood, leaning over the bank to point out the little Sticklebacks and Bullheads that lived within it, swimming in and out of some yellow plants folk called 'blobs'.

Making the girls laugh as they valiantly feigned an interest in whatever drew the lad's attention. Becoming exasperated, having to pick sticky buds out of their hair, one glance at Sal's growing irritation soon put a stop to that. Laughing fit to burst then lapsing into silence, enjoying each other's company, the trees swaying gently in the breeze, while the sun hit the water, reflecting the little mirrors of light that danced upon its surface. The odd duck waddling about near the water's edge, to waddle off again as if in fright; squawking, then dropping down into the glassy surface, splitting the mirrored light apart, to form a little wake 'til everything was still again.

*

If only they could go back, back to that, Ann would have made sure their lives took a very different course.

*

The hours rolled by the weather turned, the light upon the water changing to a deeper darker grey. Sal decided it would be best to start for home looking at the weather, Bill jumping up to walk beside her. Sally being a little better off than the three of them, living close to Skegby Manor house.

Watching their exit Ann could not help but feel a certain excitement building. Sal having taken Bill's arm it registered then, that she'd often spoken about the young man she was with, but Sal had never said one word to her about Bill. Yet it was obvious how smitten she was. All thought of that, however, went completely when moments later Jeremiah asked if he could see her home.

*

Taking his arm, recalling as if it were happening now, him placing his hand over her own and in that gesture lay a lifetime's hopes and dreams, that he would care for her always, but that was not to be.

Ann sat cherishing those memories, how they had talked of their lives, arriving quicker than she'd wanted outside the door on Bedlam Court. Considering that was how her life was running now, without any halt within its course. If only that could happen, if only you could rewind time, her eyes glistening with a thousand tears she would not shed.

Jeremiah had remarked upon them innocently once, and she'd caught the compliment like catching a shooting star that flits across the sky. For Jeremiah did not resort to gushing praise to win her; he was not the type of man for that, so Ann had locked the remark away, to remind herself of it every now and then. Remembering how respectful he always was towards her, looking down at the same fawn dress, she wore the day they met, not really listening to anything the vicar said.

If only she could walk into the world her heart resided, if only that could be.

*

"Could I see you again, we could take another walk if you would like?" He'd hesitated.

"I would like that." Another excitement had begun.

"You'll have to decide where, I've not been here long enough t' know the area that well?"

It was the first time she'd seen him unsure, but Ann already knew where. "We could go over where Sal lives, near Skegby Manor house. There's kingfishers by the little pond nearby." her reply far too quick.

"Sounds delightful." Jeremiah's eyes shone with an amusement he wasn't about to express, Ann's hurried answer a delight all of its own to him. "Unless you'd sooner the four of us?"

"No, I'd like it, just us." Overjoyed to get him to herself, knowing there were others in the town who'd spotted this enigmatic young man who looked like he belonged with the Romani's. "Hopefully you'll know how to look clever by then?"

He laughed, more sure of her feelings now. "I will do my best and call after dinner, if that's all right? Maybe see you in church in the morning?" as if to tell her it would not be the first time he had watched her there.

Glancing at the door behind which, he now knew George Bridget dwelt. Walking away with the same decisive, jaunty stride

———

17

Ann had watched so many times before, the pristine white shirt, dark waistcoat and light trousers, all the lads wore disappearing round the corner.

Opening the door Ann made an effort to creep in unnoticed, only to find her father already sat beside the fire, coughing enough to retch. He was collier, a quiet man that every night returned home black with the dust of his work, to take a bath in the large tin tub in front of the fire and settle in the same chair he now resided after eating. At the weekend he like many other miners proudly tended their tiny gardens at the back of the terraced houses, if they were lucky enough to have one, some having enough room for pigs. With little call for the "ten o' clock 'osses" then, and the waste from the pigs could be spread over the garden. Growing runner beans, vegetables and fruit, his most prized of all his sweet peas, nothing made him happier than to bring them into the house for his wife Elizabeth, knowing how much she liked them.

Looking round at Ann, George waited until she'd taken off her bonnet and his coughing let up enough for him to speak. "That lad in't shop were asking after thee t'other day, asked if I'd mind if he were t' ask thee out?"

Ann's eyes widened in horror, "What? Nathaniel Sedgwick? words tumbling from her like steam from a boiling kettle. "He spits all over the counter. I hope you said no. Tell me you said no."

Turning to drop her bonnet on the dresser that stood by the wall, there was a pause.

"Ah well, in life you'll find there's *woss' things than a bit a spit." Pretending he hadn't noticed the look of horror on her face. "Yu' could get used t' that."

"Really." Shaking her hair loose as if preening in a mirror. "Like you'd get used to smallpox I suppose." Looking for help from her sister who sat in the recess by the fire, her feet behind the coalscuttle, working on a peg rug she'd been at for months, always keeping her father company when he was home.

"Anyone that weds him not go short though will thee, wit' shop an' all." Her father paused and sniffed. "An' he not be gerrin' his sen' in trouble wi' magistrate an' the like; like some tha' knows." The statement hung in the room like it had been painted on the wall.

Ann tried to remain unmoved. "When was it you went to the shop dad? I've never seen you in a shop?"

The defiance in her tone his answer and not the one a father wanted, realising with that reaction she liked this young man he had heard a bit about already. Knowing he lodged with the Brandreths, a family of longstanding in the area, even having Brandreth Croft named after them, a few streets from Bedlam Court.

George had arrived in Sutton-in-Ashfield from Staffordshire searching for work, finding it in the mines like those he travelled with. He decided to hold fire a while and hope the romance fizzled out like those before it.

Oblivious to the undercurrent Ann's sister wasn't about to let this opportunity slip by. "He's always talking to mam. That all you want Mrs. Bridget?" Doing a very good impression, wiping her face after. "This'll be you Ann when you're wed, wiping your face all the time."

Ann looked at her, exasperation written into her expression, but nothing anyone said could alter how she felt right now.

" There's one good thing." Hannah went on. "Mrs. Sedgewick used to get a good wet cloth to wipe the counter down at end of the day, you could just use her pinny? You could wear Mrs. Sedgwick's pinny Ann. "

"Hannah, shut up, I'm not walking out with Nathaniel, he's a nice lad with a good heart, I know. When they were after the Ludd's that took the frames out the other month, Nathaniel hurried them through the shop, before the constables knew where they were. They say trades more than doubled since." Laughing. "Who'd think that?"

George lowered his head and glared at her from under his eyebrows. "An` just how'd does tha' know that?"

Ann dare not smile, but was relishing the moment. "I'm surprised you'd not heard, the pits being so full a talk. It was all over the village. You should have asked Sal, she told me." Leaving the impression she was telling him the truth.

George turned away to look into the fire, the battle already won.

Sibling rivalry though was still on the agenda. "You want to be grateful anyone wants to walk out with you, you look like you're on the Parish." A statement Hannah would regret.

Looking down Ann thawed slightly, leaving her in a dreamlike state. The dress a dirty grey along the hem and crisp white underskirt she rarely wore. Walking away from further confrontation into the back room, realising her father had a bit more information on this young man than she wanted.

Sitting in the chair wedged as usual between the fireside and the table enjoying a bit of peace and quiet, her mother sat half dozing. She was a big woman with brown grey hair pulled from her face in a bun and a steady disposition.

Opening her eyes after hearing someone come into the room, she smiled trying to gather herself, to place the bit of sewing lying idle in her hand onto the long table beside her chair. "Your father tells me you were with a young man earlier?" Wearing her mildly interested expression.

Ann felt another examination coming, yet a smile forced its way across her face, to think of Jeremiah in that way.

This alone told her mother everything she needed to know. "It would be nice if we could meet him Ann." Recognising a look she'd worn herself years ago; that was wrapped inside her heart never to leave. "If you're walking out with him, you should bring him to meet us."

"He helped me with the water that's all, there's no need for a fuss." Knowing it wasn't strictly true she hurried to the stairs, hoping to put a stop to any further interrogation.

At that moment Hannah came through holding the peg rug. "I'll call after dinner if it is all right." Smirking at her sister.

Their mother looking between them with the semblance of a smile, eyebrows raised. While Ann delivered her sister a withering glare, before proceeding up the narrow stairs to the bedroom she shared with her siblings. Wondering just how long she could hold off that meeting, knowing from previous experience her mother's gentle smile hid a steely determination.

*woss - worse

Chapter Two

A CURSE IN BROWN PAPER

Jeremiah first visited Sutton in Ashfield to look up family, on finding the town full of framework knitters the majority producing the Derby Rib; he was inclined to stay. Lodging with a realative who lived just up the road from Bedlam Court, so could not help but notice the girl with the long brown hair and stunning hazel eyes that lived there. By trade he was a framework knitter, a Shiner they were called. The seats of their trousers shone due to them sliding along the small bench at the front of the framework knitting machine and back constantly.

When Bill told him Sally's friend was always talking about him, he wasn't sure whether to believe him. Though he'd caught her looking a few times, he didn't consider she would lower herself to walk out with him. Bill had been seeing Sal a couple of weeks, but kept it to himself. Not wanting the ribbing that would go along with his friends knowing, so no one knew anything about it until Bill spilt this little nugget of information to Jeremiah. Both deciding if he went to help Ann with the water that would be the best way to introduce himself.

Things moved quickly for them, seeing each other every day since that first meeting, and moving into their own home, just up from Ann's parents straight after they were wed. Jeremiah working every hour he could in the hope of saving a little. With the need for the frame, a spinning wheel and a place for Ann to sew the garments, it took up most of one room, there was no space for all of this at Ann's parents.

Ann would sit at the table seaming the stockings; her work incredibly neat, while one of her sisters would be at the spinning wheel winding the yarn, making sure it was done properly. Everything would always go much better if there was a bit of warmth in the room, like the machine needed it, the tension on the yarn having to be just right. It took many years to be apprentice to this trade, plus the knowledge of how to mend the machines if they broke. It was strenuous work constantly pulling the carriage forward then lifting it, to take the sinkers from the needles and pull it forward again, while you had to know exactly when and where to use the foot treadles. This work needed good eyesight and plenty of daylight for the constant scrutiny that was needed to ensure nothing went amiss. Though the machine was rented you had to pay for the mending, no one had time to wait for the merchant to get around to it.

Jeremiah was often needed to help others when they realised how good he was at getting the frames running again quickly. In that way it was easy to get word around if any machines needed stopping, and no one was the wiser for it.

Everyone would know if someone happened to be working, even in the street, for the clatter of the machine was something else. Jeremiah worked as fast as the machine allowed, if you were slow it would drop stiches, taking time you hadn't got to pick them up again. It was skilled work to shape the garments, requiring you to drop loops to do it and so shape the leg, losing more toward the ankle. The stockings being made in three pieces which Ann would sew together as neatly and quickly as she could.

*

Ann remembered how kind he was but serious, too serious sometimes, for Jeremiah told her all the dreams he had; that he was thinking of a move to America for them, but first he had to save the fare. How different it was now, wishing with all her heart she'd not discouraged him for unlike Jeremiah, Ann had never been away from home. Recalling how attentive he was when she was pregnant with Elizabeth; their laughter and excitement wondering what the babe would be.

After the Luddites forced the merchants into paying the established rate again, it was the best things had been for a while. Ann was so very proud of Jeremiah and he of her, remembering his words on finding out about the babe. "I will have to save for another passage now." His smile, however, told her everything and she would always regret that she was not persuaded to consider a life many miles away, where they might have flourished.

The years went on and work was not paying as much and no amount of Luddite activity could resolve it; though they were still of a mind to try. The Luddites targeted the shoddy frames producing cut ups, work done in squares with no skill and the wide frames producing three legs at a time. Which all had the same effect, more money for the merchant and less for those working the frames. Undercutting skilled men by a distance, leaving many out of work. While the Ludd's never touched the single frames, the men with skill used, leaving notice upon those shoddy frames, that they were to stop working or face Ned Ludd. This no one minded, for though the merchants pushed the poor frames upon anyone they could, everyone realised it was in their best interests to destroy them. If anyone suffered distress due to the breaking of these frames, collections were made to see them through it; the men were always of a mind to look after their own.

A friend, Henry Sampson proposed they go together to some meetings in Nottingham, back when he and Ann were first wed, now the meetings were taking on more relevance.

There were much harsher penalties for breaking frames, the government taking on more special constables and thousands of extra soldiers to try to stop the Luddites. All drafted into Nottinghamshire, Derbyshire and the surrounding areas after the Framework Breaking Bill of 1812 passed, making it a hanging offence to break the machines. With the added military presence, it was hard to get anyone with nerve enough for a big attack. Luddite attacks were now small sharp affairs; they could not afford the mass attacks that were their previous stamp.

Jeremiah told Ann all about the speech Lord Byron gave against the Bill, delivering a blistering attack on those who considered it right. Reading her an extract from it telling Ann there was much more than that. It was Lord Byron's maiden speech in the House of Lords and the satire within it pleased those of Jeremiah's friends that read it, so he was considered a friend, but the Bill was passed anyway.

The years became a re-enactment of previous times when demand began to fall on the Derby Rib. It taking seven years to learn how to produce such work, but when times were tough it all counted for nothing. Jeremiah was always proud his work was considered among the best, but things were now upon a darker course. Like most shiners he was having to work longer and harder while Ann did the seaming and two children to look after.

In most cases the merchant not only owned the frame but the house you lived in, while the framework knitters had to buy everything, the thread, the work from the bag hosier or merchant and the mending of any breakdowns, plus the tools. When times turned you were still to pay the rent on the frame and the house. If for any reason you could not fulfill the quota of work the merchant wanted, there was a fee to pay on top and with no wage, life became harder still. Merchants were now inclined to offer payment in goods or food instead of wages, the Truck system. Some had been told there'd be no work in the future if they did not accept these terms, for there were many who'd be glad of it.

Jeremiah had been fortunate so far, but when Rueben came telling him what had happened to him, he knew his turn was coming. Taking him outside to talk, seeing that he was in no state to be near the children and not wanting Ann to overhear. Looking very dour when he came back inside, telling Ann, Reuben had been unable to produce the required amount of work. In truth

Reuben's work was never among the best and Jeremiah wondered if that was why, though his doubts were building. Making up a parcel of food he walked over to their house on Crown Lane, knowing Martha his wife was pregnant. That day Jeremiah and Ann ate only what you might give a child, Jeremiah leaving soon after to attend a meeting in Nottingham with Henry Sampson and did not come back until late.

Elizabeth, Lizzie as she was known, was now three and Timothy nearly a year, the joy Ann and Jeremiah felt in their little family was overshadowed with trade on the run from bad to worse. It was just past twelve on Saturday, when Jeremiah arrived home from the hosiery merchants with what should have been his wages. Slamming a brown paper parcel on the table, he stood like a man before the gates of Hades.

Wiping her hands on her clean white pinafore, Ann stepped from the washbowl, noting the pungent odour coming from the parcel. "What is that?" Tentatively unwrapping the paper, to see a piece of brown meat, a foul liquid oozing out over the vegetables and Ann's once pristine table. "Why have you bought that for goodness sake; I cannot give the children that." Pushing it away, as if witnessing a curse in brown paper.

Jeremiah's hands gripped the chair, his knuckles white. "You think I had a choice? It is how we are to be used and it matters little whether it's fit or not," a cold venom inside his voice Ann had never heard before.

Shocked by this change in him she could only stand and watch the truth laid out before her, realising then how he had hidden their situation, trying to protect her from it.

"If we want work, this is the payment, every hour God sends for that." Standing there 'til he could no longer hold his anger. "He said, everybody had to take their turn; an' it were mine, like he were goading me." His hands shaking so much, the chair rattled upon the floor.

Ann wanted to ease his pain, but there was nothing she could do, realising with some discomfort she'd already said enough.

"I could feel lads watchin', an' I knew why; an' what would happen, we'd hang, all on us, for that cut-purse." Swallowing. "An' him stood there, like he were some kind a better than us, the man is no more than a thief. I'd seen specials waitin' round back if aught kicked off. I knew… I knew that they were there. All while he were looking at me, almost laughin'. Pictures flashed in front a' me, a' lad's done for Ludding, Jem Towle, an' others hanging there, an' I could see 'um, plain as day. There were nothing I could do…so, I walked." Closing his eyes, his chest heaving up and down as if a bellows.

Ann realised then how close she'd been to losing him, while she went happily about her chores, none of it seemed real. Having always faced their situation with resolve and even harder work, Jeremiah had fooled her into believing things would change.

Now he stood unable to look in her direction, trying to gather himself, until he exploded with anger again. "While he buys that little un' of his another pony to ride across our common, to go wi'

the three they have already. An' all on us, we cannot feed our
little un's. An' he thinks that's *rate, rate to do to folk." Turning
to her suddenly, his breathing laboured. "You know that common
we grazed animals on, the one that's his now 'cause he says so,
'cause he's fenced the bugger off." While we starve an' cannot
even take a rabbit wi' out 'um after us. 'Tis us the rabbits now,
while he screws us for every blasted penny and more. An' they
know how we are fixed; they know." The fire within those eyes
not so warm and tender now, it was then he appeared to melt
before her. Without warning turning off, to pull his jacket from
the chair, the door slamming behind him enough to take it from its
hinges.

Ann did not know how long she stood trying to gather herself.
Grabbing the parcel she ran the few yards down the street to see if
there was anything to be done. Timothy shocked and silent, Lizzie
clinging to her dress, all three wondering what was happening in
their world. Going in the back way, knowing her mother would
be there.

Elizabeth took one look and motioned to the chair, having heard
talk things had taken a turn weeks ago. "Sit down." Taking the
parcel from her and glancing at it; screwing up her face. "You sit
there, an` quiet them little un's." Walking into the front room,
where George was bent upon the mending of his boots, papers all
laid out across the floor.

Ann listened, her father's hammering stopped. Timothy's crying
half hiding their muffled talk, her mother, 'telling him to leave

things be,' the hammering started up again with more conviction, then the door was put too.

Ann sat like she'd been bolted to the chair, staring out of the window at the frames her father used for his runner beans, that weren't doing so well this year. Starting to rock back and forth but quaking inside, trying to calm the children, Timothy clinging to her with a force that belied his age, saying over and over. "Dada, Dada."

Lizzie stood beside her sucking in her lips, trying to get up onto her knee. Putting her arm about her, Ann stroked her hair to calm her, doing exactly what her husband always did to soothe her.

It wasn't long till Elizabeth bustled through the door, a picture of calm motherly assurance. Placing a fresh brown paper parcel onto the table, she hurried around it, to place the old iron *brandreth to the fire and plant the kettle over it, a sigh issuing from her, considering the iron stand well named. "Where's Jeremiah?"

The distress was now too much for Ann.

Elizabeth lifted Timothy instantly, ushering her granddaughter before her into the front room, then hurried back.

While, Ann looked into her mother's eyes as if for absolution. "I don't know; he thought I were blaming him, an` I didn't mean to… I've never seen him like it, a bit cross, but not like that. He walked out. An' I don't know…" Unable to continue, wiping her hands across her face, her voice trembling. "I saw Jessie other day, you know Jessie? Her husband's gone, an` she's no-one, an' four little un's not nine yet. Merchant said she had to be out of her house, or they'd throw her out. Lord knows what's going to happen, an' her wi' them babes. Said there was naught else she could do but workhouse. An` I know I've you, but… if I'd no one, that'd be me. An' they won't pay her that much no matter how hard she works, 'cause she's just doin' extra seamin'." Dissolving into tears. "He never said how bad he were feeling 'til now, not a word. I thought it would all come right in the end." Wiping her hands over her face again, trying to hide the tears.

Elizabeth said nothing, her lips pressed tight together like her granddaughter's, walking over to the drawer under the washbowl, to find a handkerchief.

Spinning around when George walked in holding Timothy.

Looking between them jogging the little boy up and down, singing the rhyme the children liked, "the woodpecker cried 'god bless my soul, take it out, take it out, oh blimey," while his granddaughter remained in the other room by her Aunt helping with the rug.

Elizabeth passed a cup of tea to both of them, George sitting himself at the table placing Timothy upon it, making faces at him, the dark eyes watching every little move, starting to laugh again.

Drying her tears, Ann clung to the warmth of the cup as if it held the cure to all her ills.

"Stop tha' fretting, we will pull together like folk do, Jeremiah's a proud lad I know, an' Jessie is staying at Mrs. Stone's, I saw her when I were coming back, she's taken that rank bit a meat."

———

Elizabeth shook her head. "Said she could do somethin' with it, saw me throwing it away. I told her to chuck it, but she insisted. Stop worrying over Jessie she'll have a bad stomach if she eats it mind, but she couldn't be told. Mrs. Stones will have it from her well, I nipped in an' told her too. Go home, an' cook that lad a thine something to eat, he'll be back, he'll not leave thee."

Ann got up to stand beside the table, putting the cup down, not having drunk any of it, unwrapping the biggest cut of meat she'd seen in a while and a whole week's worth of vegetables." Turning to thank her mother.

Elizabeth spun away to rattle the poker at the fire; her tears were not to be shed in front of those that needed her.

Picking up Timothy Ann hurried up the little street, looking at the clouds flying across the sky like someone chased them, wishing she could follow. Timothy cuddling against his mothers neck, dropping to sleep, while Lizzie stayed by her Aunt Hannah doing her best to help and quite good having little fingers. The colour pattern Hannah had set her heart upon wasn't quite going to plan, however, but she bore with it, knowing her sister never cried and lord knows she'd pushed her enough,

George looked at his wife, waiting for the door to close, not wanting Ann or anyone else to overhear, Elizabeth settled opposite cup in hand. "Jeremiah takes things hard; truth is I cannot see an end to it." Shaking his head. Other day I were comin` along Beggar Street, you know that little shop, on't end, the one that used t' sell them Sugar plums we had last Christmas,

<hr>

an` them fancy twelfth cakes the' make for t' rich folk. Cost a fortune, them Sugar Plums can you 'member, but look on their faces when the' had 'um." George's smile drifted away. "Ah well, they'll be no more, the' were boarding it up, said no one went any more. Mind I'm not surprised at them prices." Starting to cough again.

Elizabeth's recollection of it turned to worry, shaking her head. "It were Isaiah served me with meat, I told him what had happened, an' he just looked at me, said. 'We've known each other a while eh Lizbet.' You know how he calls me that. Then he smiled, an' said," stopping to gather herself. "If I cannot help proper folk when there's need, I'll be damned. I've heard thee makin' folk take food not fit t' eat, like that's a wage for a week's work; that's not rate is it, give that lass a thine this.' Then he gave me the meat, well I must a looked like I'd been struck, God knows how I didn't cry." Dabbing her eyes. "Mansfield's that bad there's folk lying in't street, workhouse there's burstin'."

George put his hand over his wife's, to give it a squeeze and smiled. "We'll ha' to manage, an' we will, we'll get through. I asked at pit; but the' were nothing. Didn't say ought `cos I didn't want to raise lad's hopes." Letting out a sigh, he got up, finished off his tea, placing his mug back upon the table, to take his jacket from the chair. "I'll not be long, might take a turn about." George was off to thank Isaiah, then take a bit of air and see if he could find Jeremiah.

*

Like everywhere else in 1816 nothing much had grown like it should. Mount Tambora had erupted the year earlier, thousands of miles away in Indonesia, causing huge changes in the weather and decimating crops, adding to the desperate plight of those without.

Many considered the end of the world was upon them, even in Italy in the hottest months of the year, frost and dense fog hung over the land without moving, turning summer into winter.

*

It was well past midnight when Jeremiah arrived home. Ann lay within a bed that felt much too big for her without him, waiting for his arrival. Tears drenching the pillow, just grateful he was home and safe. Never having felt the distance between them she felt now, like she could see him there but couldn't reach him. Hearing the plate being taken from the large iron pot beside the fireplace Ann had used, wanting to keep it warm then placed onto the table, praying it was still good enough to eat.

Eventually she heard him coming up the stairs, the floorboards creaking when he went into the other room to check upon the children like he always did. A ritual that usually annoyed her was now a source of comfort, knowing he was still the husband she adored.

Without her realising he was so close, gently moving back the covers, to see she was not asleep at all.

Finding his anger had caused more distress than he wanted, the tables turned and he was desperate to make amends. "Ann, I

---

should never of raised my voice, none of it is your fault. An' I would do anything to make it right."

There was a sigh that pierced her heart from his, turning to him. "Neither is it yours, everyone's the same things will change; and we will manage till they do."

He settled beside her, Ann pulling herself toward him to hold him so very tight, wanting to ease the burden she knew weighed so heavily upon him.

Jeremiah smiled and not for the first time realised how much he needed her, but deep inside he could not see a future for them, no matter where he looked. Knowing with a dreadful certainty it would only be a matter of time until they had no work at all.

Next morning, they were up early; Jeremiah was his usual self after going to church and discussing things with others in the same position. Once back home after producing dinner Ann took off her shoes and sat herself beside the table to distract the children. Who were unable to understand why they couldn't have the food that was placed strategically out of their reach. With the amount they had been given, Ann could make it last a while if she were strict about it. On occasion Jeremiah would rise from the table and put whatever he had left on his plate onto theirs. With crops failing due to the dreadful weather and bread more expensive than any framework knitter could afford, all they could do was hang onto the hope that work would pick up enough to earn a decent living once again.

All the shops within the little town were struggling except one, and that had queues around the block, with folk waiting to pawn whatever they had; in the hope of furnishing their families with something more to eat. Everyone finding it hard; with nothing left for clothes or shoes. It was so bad folk were keeping their children from Sunday school for the shame they felt, Sunday school being the only schooling they would get.

It went on and on in this way, the anger and resentment Jeremiah felt having to accept the truck system and take payment in food or goods, was to embed itself into his soul, that payment never the value of the work.

A few weeks later it was still a blow when no one wanted the Derby rib at all. Jeremiah walked home feeling sick inside, not wanting the children or Ann to see him in a state again.

Opening the door, he smiled but hadn't the courage to tell Ann, walking out again to nowhere in particular. Going mile after mile, finding his way back by asking folk he passed, and always the same question, if they knew of any work, but the answer he so wanted never came.

He was no nearer a solution when he had sight of home. What was he to say to Ann, that he could no longer feed them, a man with no worth at all was how he saw himself, knowing others were in the same situation did not help? He stood a distance from the dam were they'd first walked out together with Bill and Sally in a much happier time than this.

This place, somehow, seemed to share the bleakness of his life, trees moved back and forth to cast their shadow on the water.

Understanding now why men walked out upon their family, to end this sense of shame and inadequacy that had fallen on him like a stone.

If they'd needed soldiers, he would have returned to that, but the war with France was over, those who served were all in his position. While the pits had lists of men waiting for work, more than they would ever need, it was the same with farming.

The small amount he'd put by for his dream of a new life in America would disappear like rain into the River Idle. He stood watching the moonlight drift through the clouds, to play a moment on the waters surface. Cauldwell Dam lay below like a mirrored doorway to release, silently pulling you toward its secrets, secrets only it could know, a darkness closing upon him.

Shaking himself, he fixed his clothing and was about to walk away, next to the bank where huge boughs overhung the water, lay a heap of rags, and then he ran. To reach the water's edge and fight against the branches eager to keep what they had gained, wading up to his waist to pull the body from their clutches and up onto the bank.

The knowledge of who it was came before he ever reached the water. A man who loved his family driven through despair to this, the fear and shame that haunted their lives was now starting to defeat them.

He sat upon the bank as if it were a summer's day, tears rolling down his face. Talking to a friend, one of the best he'd ever known, a man who he'd relied on, who would never tell his secrets, he would remain and always be the staunchest of them all. Remembering when they'd met upon the Green, talking over how the night before had gone, how Alf told him then "he would all' is ha' his back," when they went in to smash the frames. Wishing he had done the same for Alf or at the very least seen his pain and known how he was feeling, they were in the same position, so why hadn't he shared this with him, he would never know the answer.

Well the merchants had their revenge and more besides, not once though, had they ever killed a man. There had been one of their number shot and killed at one encounter and if they'd reached the men responsible, who knows what would have happened. The frame owners barricaded themselves upstairs, so the lads had hacked at the ceiling, until they'd pulled it down around them, once upstairs however those brave frame owners were nowhere to be seen.

Now there were men not knowing where to turn, Alf Lawrence would not be the only man to find his own path out of this. Heartening himself with the only good he could see, at least he was found and Jessie could mourn her man. Stockingers Rest had claimed another and all he could do was hope Alf rested the easier for it. If he ever thought of doing the same, he now saw the mistake. Would Alf rest easy, for Jeremiah knew how Jessie loved him and the next day someone else's shame would stand where Alf's had been. Nothing, though, could bring him back to those who loved for him; those gaping wounds would never heal.

———

Trying to offer some measure of respect he tidied Alf the best he could. Then walked to Rueben's to get help, bringing Joe with them, seeing that he was there, after another row with his long suffering wife, Joe was inclined to play the field. There wasn't a word between them when they carried Alf back to his wife and family. Mrs. Stones appearing at the door a huge shawl wrapped around her, turning off to fetch Jessie, then hurrying to get them all something warm to drink. It was then that Jess broke, crying for what seemed hours over her husbands body, while they stood head bowed beside a tiny babe who joined her mothers crying, while the rest of Jessie's children lay clothed in sleep.

 When Jeremiah finally arrived home that night, he could not find the courage to tell Ann anything about it and fell into bed beside her.

Jeremiah's pride had taken such a beating he had no option but accept the situation, for he had seen the road ahead, but that night had hardened him and little did he know the following days would offer no reprieve.

Forced onto parish relief along with hundreds more, with help from Ann's parents they were getting by. Parish relief, however, couldn't cope with the numbers, being funded by those with work and for every household in work; there were eight without in Sutton.

 Every day Jeremiah and Ann would leave the children with her mother and go over to the workhouse, to find most of the town there. Jessie would sit next to Ann to do her seaming and bring her eldest along to wind the yarn. Maud having taken losing her father very hard indeed, now wouldn't let Jess out of her sight, while the babe would cry pitifully beside them in a tiny wicker basket.

Jessie was all but skin and bone, every so often she would turn off to feed the little bundle, which had no effect at all upon the crying. Everyone looking at one another wishing they could help, but with no wet nurse spare in the neighbourhood there was little to be done. A few of the girls brought things in to try upon the babe, but the tiny thing was like her mother and refused everything they offered. Even Mrs. Dove the mistress of the workhouse brought some goats milk in to try upon the infant, and a small tincture someone said would get her going, but it was all to no avail.

The sound of the machines would then drown out the crying, for the place was wall to wall with lines of frames, everyone working for the few shillings they received from Thomas Dove the Master of the Workhouse who was not as strict as some. It had been erected the year previous not far from Bedlam Court, Jeremiah never thinking he would ever be inside it.

By the afternoon he would be off trying to find work, coming back with Rueben, Joe and a rabbit or pheasant besides, but never any work. If they'd been caught, it would have been seven years transportation; poaching with a net received the same penalty as if you were using a gun.

Those with money enough had been allowed to buy up common

land, where ordinary folk grazed cattle or trapped a rabbit or two, which helped in times like this. Those that held this new bounty employed a good number of gamekeepers to make sure any poachers were caught and the full force of the law applied.

On these days Ann would walk from the workhouse with Jess and Maud, collect the children from her mother and worry over where her husband was? Yet it seemed to give Jeremiah a perverse sort of satisfaction, much like his meetings and the game was very welcome.

It was no surprise to anyone when a few days later Martha hurried over to tell Ann, before they started work that Jessie would be late, her youngest was failing and word went quickly round the workhouse.

Jessie arrived after a few hours, little Maud beside her, her face devoid of all expression, so everyone could guess the news.

Ann lent across, when Jess was settled, "I am so sorry Jess." There was no reply, moving a little closer on seeing how her hands were trembling. "Just pretend you're working, we will do your shift, if the seaming is not straight, they will not pay you."

Mouthing this at Martha, who sat a few rows on beside Rueben, no one having the time for getting up, there was a quota to be done, so lip reading was preferred to get a message through. Jess just closed her eyes and nodded, staring at the seaming as if it might be inclined to jump up and do itself. A few girls stopped to help Jessie, so within a couple of hours it was all done, helping to feed what was left of her family.

———

Mrs Dove coming to stand beside them, to see what it was all about, but said naught. Then stomped off down the alleyway between the rows of frames; Ann turned to look at Martha, eyebrows raised, hoping they'd still get paid the full amount. Afterwards they walked together arm in arm, down Back Lane, Jessie in the middle, young Maud holding her mother's hand so tight Ann wasn't sure exactly who needed it most. It was only then Ann noticed Maud had no shoes at all, and by the looks of it, it had been that way a while, which hit her like she'd received a blow, long skirts could hide such things it seemed. Getting to Mrs. Stones, to see what help they could be, for Jessie wasn't up to much.

The little wicker basket had been placed upon the table in the middle of the room, a white cloth wrapped around the babe, and a few flowers beside it.

Mrs. Stones herself a tall well-dressed woman who was very good with a needle, had made it very pretty. Taking Ann to one side, to tell her 'Jessie hadn't been able to feed the infant what with Alf gone and was now giving her food to the children. She'd tried her to encourage her, not wanting anything else to happen and the children be without their mother, but Jessie didn't seem to have the inclination'.

Someone knocked upon the door and one of Jessie's children Job, hurried to it. Rueben and Jeremiah stood upon the doorstep to be asked inside. Walking towards Ann, Jeremiah then went across to Jessie to put his arm about her, while Rueben nodded to all within the room.

Seeing how Jess was, and after speaking to Mrs. Stones he decided to go over to old Harry's. "We will see what can be done."

Rueben went for the door knowing exactly what this meant, for babes were often buried alongside another body if you could persuade the gravedigger, with else no-one the wiser and no cost, helping those who'd not the money for a burial.

Jeremiah gave Jess another hug, then strode off with Rueben, once outside he looked up into the clouds, hoping Alf could see and would approve. Wondering where it all would end or if it ever would.

Returning quickly for it was not far, nodding to Mrs. Stones who gathered everyone round the table to hold a little service of their own. Now at least the tiny babe would rest in consecrated ground, after Jess began thanking Rueben and Jeremiah over and over when they told her not to worry that it would go ahead that day. After their little service Jess gently bent to kiss the tiny babe, and turned away. Mrs. Stones gathered the children again to pray beside their mother, for Jess could not watch another member of her family leave.

Jeremiah gently wrapped a woolen shawl around the basket and strode off with Rueben. Towards the gravedigger's shed where Harry would always wait for proceedings to commence, fortunately there was a burial that afternoon. Mrs. Stones had connections and would speak to those who dealt with these things, for she was well acquainted with them.

Lack of food and infection was starting to take its toll upon the town, so the little boxes were found more frequently, left just inside the church, in the hope old Harry would feel inclined to do his best.

No-one wanted to know where these boxes came from, but they were never left upon the north side of the church, for that doorway was thought to be where evil spirits left the building.

A few of days later Ann felt a joyous lift in spirits when she turned the corner to go over to the cottage, to see Nathaniel knock upon the door, carrying a box of food, a wooden toy on top and a pair of shoes fitting for an eight year old, Mrs. Stones, ushering him inside, so Ann decided not to bother with her visit.

The grip poverty had upon the town now began to take a firmer hold, so many were on parish relief both Ann and Jeremiah knew their removal order would not be long in coming. The parish being unable to feed all who were in need, under the Poor Law those born outside the parish, were required to move back to the parish of their birth, whether they wanted to or not.

Jeremiah was born in Holborn, London, but he was never going to say so to the overseer, his family having moved to Exeter, when he was in his teens. He had been sent to school there enlisting in the army at seventeen. Only moving to Nottingham when his parents died, which gave him the opportunity to say it was his place of birth.

When the warrant for their removal arrived at Bedlam Court,

Ann did her best to hide her feelings. Gathering every item, while family and friends huddled round to see them off, after helping pack their possessions. Everyone hugging Ann and the little ones time and again, telling them they would visit when they could. Timothy was having fun pulling his face at all the kissing he was having to endure; a reaction Ann's brother taught him, that was making everyone laugh. Especially when Ann snatched him up to curtail his impudence, for Ann knew the thoughts of those stood about were with them, but the visits were unlikely.

Ann's parents were standing to one side like they were made of wood, trying to smile, at this the most distressing moment of their lives. Elizabeth was suddenly taken with a desire to rush away at odd intervals, thinking of something else Ann could not do without. 'Til George had to physically restrain her, at which point a small argument ensued.

A chorus of good wishes started echoing about them, Ann's mother turning away in floods of tears that were not to witnessed by man, beast or neighbour, and in a moment they were gone.

When they were lost from sight, Elizabeth took to standing in the middle of the road, like they might without warning reappear, 'til George put his arm about her to guide her back into the house.

*rate – right.

*brandreth – iron trivet, used in cooking for placing pans or kettle upon.

*Cut-purse –Thief.

Chapter Three

IF WE MAKE IT SO

After an uncomfortable ride, Jeremiah told the Parish overseer that Nottingham had been his place of birth, and after some deliberation they found themselves in the overcrowded buildings not far from the canal on Butchers Close.

The move was four months ago, and when they first arrived Jeremiah hoped he might find work. Any he did find lasted a few of days and paid little, Nottingham it seemed was not much different to Sutton for the work.

Ann, though, began to think her husband took some purpose from the move with the meetings he attended, while she could only feel the loss of family and Sal.

Sal had lived next door on Bedlam Court, until her parents inherited a smallholding, so times were not so tight for Sal.

It wasn't long after their arrival they began to sell a few bits and pieces, to get more food and shoes for Lizzie. Over a period of time all they had left were a couple of rickety chairs no one wanted and a bed that was thankfully big enough for them all. Which helped when trying to keep warm, not having enough blankets to sleep separately anyhow.

Embarrassed by this turn in their fortunes Ann could not contemplate inviting Sal and Bill to their bare room, not that it was that much better when they had more furniture. For every time they lit a fire, damp would run down the blackened walls. While the grate within the fireplace lay half broken, with no pot-hooks for cooking, until Sal brought over different sized hooks on her visit, after Ann had mentioned there were none in a letter. Which Bill took to carting along like he was jangling a set of keys, much to Sal's annoyance and their amusement. Bill unperturbed by any of it, more than used to Sal's airs and graces to be bothered.

Instead of inviting them to their squalid room, Ann tried to pretend it wasn't quite so bad by ask Jeremiah to write. Then they would then meet them off coach, but could count upon two fingers how often it happened and felt herself wilt a little every day because of it. Not wanting to lose a friendship that meant so much to her.

Without seeing the conditions in which they lived, Sal considered they might have other friends when no further letters came; but Sal's world was not their own, while Bill was still Bill and oblivious to all of it.

After these visits Ann and Jeremiah would sit in contemplation of the life they used to have, feeling more estranged from it than ever. To lift her spirits Ann would take the children to the leafy gardens where refined folk paraded up and down, along Leen side opposite the warehouse on the wharf. Withdrawing into the world she now inhabited, too ashamed to do more. Not going too far into these gardens for fear folk would look askance at her, as if the plague of poverty could be transmitted through the air.

The blank stare she'd witnessed on arrival was now hers, to lift her beyond the insignificant folk, who cared little and knew

———

48

nothing of her life, folk who could have petitioned for reform, but wouldn't. Choosing instead to cling to some banal reasoning, always certain if they found themselves in such a situation they'd be able to find work, or those with money enough not to care.

Ann smiled, but it was pity that she felt, that they could not feel for those in need. How she wished them all inside her world and if rebellion fell upon them, could her life get any worse.

On occasion, she would meet someone in her situation, in a quiet corner of the gardens. Mother's with children whose shoes needed mending and clothes worn through, stitched up the best a mother could, then the world did not feel quite so judgmental.

*

After spending the better part of the day in the workhouse, Ann would return to their little room with the children, while Jeremiah would go in search of work. Coming home he'd often be more of a hindrance than help, either in a studious silence that went on and on, or he'd excite the children so much they would not settle then to sleep. There seemed no in between, the in between Ann longed for and hoped one day would return. Once when they were quarreling he had said and she remembered it now, if he could not feed or clothe them, at least they knew he loved them and a piece of him came back to her. Remembering the day so vividly when her world had spun away from her.

The silences became more frequent and his temper was not held as easy as before, not with her or the children, but a million other things.

When Jeremiah did find work, usually mending someone else's frames, he would come home the man she loved, with the gentle light in his eyes. Relieved that he could feed his family again, hoping things were about to change. Then he would spend his night sitting on the broken chair by the fire teaching Elizabeth to read small words he'd written on the back of his hand. While Timothy would stand behind him in the chair, hanging about his father's shoulders, jumping up and down when Lizzie happened to get one right.

On one such occasion after they had argued he'd returned home with flowers from the meadow just across the river, remembering her birthday. Ann placed them in the tiny blackened window, the sunlight shining bright behind them, showing her why love was seen the clearer when it was viewed beside despair.

Being out of work Jeremiah could regularly attend the Hampden Club meetings that started up last year, where they would talk of reform and the petitioning of parliament, hoping it would provide help to those suffering distress. Going on to the assemblies where Gravenor Henson, the leader of the framework knitters, would address them, discussing the established rates and the improvements that were needed.

Ann could not help but think when told, that a day's work would be an improvement, never mind established rates.

Henry Sampson the friend who'd invited Jeremiah to these meetings years ago was friendly enough, but Ann was never keen on him. Jeremiah was convinced Ann didn't like him because the meetings took him from his family and maybe he was right.

On these occasions, Ann had found herself a friend, their neighbours were supporters of reform, Alexander Amos's wife was a friendly woman and just what Ann needed to stop her fraying nerves. Thankful she had someone just along the passage when Jeremiah left the squalid little room, often coming over for a chat.

It was in January, Jeremiah came to tell her the Hampden Clubs were putting a petition together to go before Parliament, calling for the right to vote for every man. All hoping this would be the breakthrough that was needed, with radicals like Sir Francis Burdett and Henry Hunt backing it.

The end result, though, when it came was like every other appeal to help the poor, it was thrown out by a vote of over two to one.

After this petition was turned down, stones were hurled at the King's coach as it went by, within that crowd a man named William Richards. The same William Richards who later used the alias 'William Oliver,' the government pointed to this incident as reason enough in March to suspend Habeas Corpus, so men could now be gaoled without trial for however long the government wanted.

Unrest was on the rise; a march had been instigated from Lancashire, named after those taking part, all travelling with a blanket on route to London. The Blanketeers hoped to put a petition before the Prince Regent about the distress they suffered.

Thousands gathered to see them off, ignoring the fact they'd been read the riot act, they set off in small groups and determined fashion. Not getting too far before being dispersed by Cavalry; although the marchers were unarmed, some were said to have sustained sabre wounds. One man managed to get to London so they'd heard but did not know if that was true.

Then along came the 'Seditious Meetings Act', brought in to stop gatherings of over fifty, now things appeared to be on the road from bad to worse. They'd heard from Bill and Sally that card games, the like of Sutton Brag were no longer to be tolerated within the alehouses, along with dancing or anything contrary to common law back home. Though Jeremiah had not the money for the alehouse, he knew it was much the same in Nottingham from his meetings. There was to be no joy at all it seemed for working folk, not that many had the money for it.

Meetings had to be much more secretive, many believed ordinary folk had no rights at all. Even then it wasn't until all the new draconian rules were imposed that the Hampden Club meetings turned to a graver course. Many considered their only chance now was to overthrow the government to help those in the direst need.

Jeremiah came home to Ann saying he could see no other course and there was talk of a rising. Announcing that if it was to happen he would stand with them, for he could see no hope without it. Word came through there was a new delegate who had been around the circuit, assuring them London was also ready to join the fight for reform.

All the women so Mrs. Amos said, thought it would come to nothing like everything before it; but it appeared to be happening after all.

How were they to know who could and could not be trusted? That the Government not only watched and waited, but were determined a rising of some sort should go ahead, so they could then put on a show trial and terrify the populace into dismissing all thoughts of reform altogether. Things could then stay exactly the way they were; this poverty did not touch them, why should they care.

*

Jeremiah sat by the hearth his arm round Lizzie, every now and then a tiny blue flame leapt forward, bending he pointed to it. "Look Lizzie it is a sprite, if you wish hard enough, she makes your dreams come true, but you must not touch her or ask too much, for she will hurt you, she is not always kind."

Gazing at them huddled together, Ann shook her head; his tales always had a nip at the end of them.

Lizzie's eyes were now shining into his, a quick look at her mother as if appealing for her help, "I wished for a pony Dada and I've been good, you said so." Using the name her brother called him, jumping up and down, then slapping her hands excitedly upon his leg, while the shadows played upon the blackened walls.

Lifting his little girl when the fire began to spit, to sit her upon his knee, her long brown hair so like her mother's. Smiling at her

her persistence, wanting the rhyme he would amused her with, so started to jog her up down, pretending she rode the pony she wanted. The pony he always promised, but could never quite deliver, a rhyme he recited every night. Ladies go nim, nim nim, gently jogging her up and down, gentlemen go joggity, joggity, slightly faster, until he got to farmers go gallopty, gallopty, at which he would bounce Lizzie up and down with much more vigour. Until she was unable to speak, she was laughing so much, then he would cradle her into his lap until she settled there for sleep. While he wished with all his being he could provide for his family and not be reliant on the parish. Never thinking he'd be in this position, unable to see a way clear. The area they lived so squalid children did not play within these streets; they would stand and stare like apparitions, at a world that didn't care.

Nottingham's slums stood testament to decay, haunted shells of what they should have been, yet within those walls lived folk who shared everything they had. He sat cradling his little girl, an anger swelling inside of him, obliterating all the good he held.

Knowing nothing of these thoughts Ann gently took Lizzie from him, seeing she was half asleep. Gently placing her beside her brother, already slumbering peacefully, returning to sit opposite.

"Only man that spoke for us was Byron an' he's chased out a t' country with some scandal or other, no doubt made up. God knows why that Chaworth girl whatever her name is, married Jack Musters, she'll regret that, sure as night follows day. Came that night we took frames out, just after we were wed. Prancing up an'

down when all lads had gone, frames all over place all way t'
Frameworker's. I were sat outside, Bill were wi' me, we'd just
been in yard to wash dirt off us faces. 'Asked if we'd seen aught?'
I said we'd just come an' were shocked at mess.' He turned an'
rode off, the' were little un's runnin' after him shoutin' an'
throwin' stuff. Bill just about managed to hold his sen' from
laughing, never were any good at that sort a thing. They say they
have more informers now, well he'll bloody well need 'um."

Jeremiah shoved the poker at the fire, falling silent. "Be better
for us if he'd stayed. I'm sure on it. Saw him once goin' along top
road, must a been two year ago now, maybe three, when it were
first up for sale, Newstead I mean, asked how it were goin'? I just
looked at him. Then I thought nah, I'll share glad tidings. He said
naught, an' I thought here's another, all spit an' nought else. Then
he said 'how sorry he were, that were t' case,' gave me what he
had hanging off saddle; brace a pheasants, beauties an' all.

The' say he's always trying to make him sen out a Dandy.
It were t' way he laughed after, like it were an act though. He
were a bit different like, with fancy frilly shirt an' a face scrubbed
like you'd gone o'er it with a yard brush. Far as I know he were
no Dandy when he were at boxing club. That were a dirty hole
that were, he didn't care, seemed to enjoy it, he could drink mind,
didn't remember me, an' I weren't in't mood to remind him. Just
looked at him, in't end I had to say some at so I thanked him for t'
speech, he made in House a Lord's. Can remember thinking, I
were not myself, but he'd give me birds so I thought I ought to.

—

He just shrugged. 'If only it had changed their minds. A very good day to you Sir.' Turned horse an' were off. He were only man among 'um apart from reformers. Went into prison round that time to see Major Cartwright when they arrested him, took him a load a books an' stuff. Bloody man were eighty odd; shoved him about an' the lot, from all accounts, cause he were having a meeting with our side. Byron kicked up a fuss again in a speech, caused um' more embarrassment."

Deciding not to tell Ann about the other things he'd heard. Beside one of the maids, who worked at Newstead falling pregnant to him; it had been the talk of all around that he'd settled a hundred pounds a year on her, as well as the child, 'til she went off with his page, so dropped her money to half after that.

"I told Alf, he said he were always handin' stuff out t' folk, if he'd got aught on him. Unlike him we've got at Hardwick, Duke a ruddy Devonshire, he's more like to run you down. Remember when he came through, when he first got Hardwick, in that big fancy coach, when it were his coming of age celebration at Hall, cause he didn't like Chatsworth. We ought to a' tipped him out an' into pond, that had a been a surprise rate enough for him, cooled him down a bit," looking into the fire as if for answers.

Ann laughed, but said nothing, feeling much more tired than usual, leaning against the wall to let the fire warm her, no matter what it was like outside, these buildings were never warm, thankful the children were settled. Having felt this sort of tired twice before, but not sure enough to say and did not want to 'til she was; it was the last thing they needed.

Wondering if Jeremiah was now considering the consequences if this march went ahead. Knowing the fire within would never be quelled 'til there was change, having seen it so many times before. In reality she thought things would blow over, though it wouldn't change their situation one jot. "Are they still of a mind to march?"

"Aye times are set, I've another meeting, then we will show them where they stand." His eyes took on a steely glare. "Last week four were arrested and taken to Derby gaol for setting fire t' a couple a' hayricks over South Wingfield way. The' did it 'cause Colonel Wingfield Halton, man that owned 'um had thrown folk out a their houses onto t' street. They will hang them Ann, in all honesty do they need t' hang them? They have no pity for the likes of us; we are like insects t' them, to be crushed underfoot, with no more thought either and God willing the day will soon be here when we will show them the error of that."

Ann had always known Jeremiah had been a Luddite, smashing the frames that put good men out of work, but this was different. He was just past thirty, young and brave with a wild romantic look about him, that so captivated her when she first met him. Sometimes too driven by his sense of what was right for his own good, but fearless in the face of what he considered an injustice. Ann loved him for all of it, indeed, if her husband put his mind to anything he would not rest until he'd seen it through. Maybe that's why he felt so aggrieved when he couldn't find the work.

Realising now this might go ahead after all she could not quell her fear, nor her eyes conceal it.

Jeremiah smiled and crouched before her; placing his hands over her own. "Ann I cannot let them march without me. It is bad enough I cannot feed us. I would not feel a man if I let them stand alone." Seeking to ease her fears, cradling her face with his hand. "I cannot stay while they fight Ann, how can I? They need men who have dealt with such before." Showing the same tenderness he always did. For Jeremiah loved his family, it was for them he wanted change, so they had a better life than this.

Trying to get the courage from somewhere Ann returned his smile.

"Haven't I always come back to you Ann? And I will come back this time, you will see and if we make it so, our lives will be the better for it. If it is the way we've planned, things will change in time. Have faith, for right is with us, no one should live like this. There are those with wealth more than they can spend, made off the back of folk they work into the ground and do not pay a proper wage. All we want is work and proper payment; a say in the running of this land, is it so wrong to want that? There are thousands marching, I am but a cog inside a giant wheel, you will see when we arrive in Nottingham, it will rise to greet us, there are so many desperate for change."

Ann seemed heartened by his words. "You are mine, that is all I care, I could not love you more."

Jeremiah smiled, his eyes shining into hers and as the fire receded in the grate, they settled beside the children for the night.

———

Over the next few days Jeremiah could not settle his mind to anything. In the evening he had taken to walking by the canal trying to consider what was right. Tonight was no exception, making his way for once slowly towards the meeting place. Pondering what would happen if they did not get the outcome they desired, what hope was there for him. The darkest thoughts overtook him, the thoughts he never shared with Ann. Before this enterprise began hope had been so hard to find.

He stood considering his options; Ann and the children would have family to care for them. Though he had never said so to her, it seemed the only way for him. To overthrow this government might in the end bring work. If not, all he offered those he loved was a life of squalid indignity. In truth lately he often thought Ann would be better off without him, maybe find someone who could give her all that he could not. All he did was shackle his family to a half-life, he looked wistfully at the canal, watching the water racing by. Out of nowhere a chill swept from the water like a mist, to wrap itself around him. An image rose, to stare as if transfixed. He tried to shake this vision, but a cold sweat swelled inside, to sink deep into his bones. The spectre suddenly sat bolt upright, as if in a convulsion before death, shaking its head this way and that, to disappear as though it had never been there at all, the image of a friend had left an imprint on him that could not be forgotten and was to haunt him so it seemed. If he could speak to Alf right now he would tell him firmly it was something he could do without.

He stood as if frozen, struggling to gain enough presence of mind to turn away, another vision. Unable to rally his senses and remove the grip this spectre had upon him. Shaking, he walked hurriedly away, pulling the brown greatcoat tight about him that would not close, for he was unable to afford fastenings, fixing his hat to shiver once again, and rub his hands up and down the grey trousers he always wore, in an effort to gain warmth and dislodge the image, managing through it all of it to make himself late.

Striding through the narrow streets going directly to the inn in the centre of Nottingham across the market place. Looking at the old man sat in the corner who nodded, so proceeded down the steps to the back-room door.

There was an audible sigh of relief when he entered the darkened room, a few candles dotted here and there.

Thomas Bacon walked across to grasp him by the hand. "Thought you weren't coming." Walking over to the hatch thumping his fist on it, turning to him with a smile. The blackened timbers of the room making it appear far darker than it was.

Jeremiah said nothing, just set him with a look of mild amusement. Then went to stand beside the fire hoping to shake the eerie feeling that just would not leave him be, drifting away after a time, amid a sea of hope that swelled and ricocheted about the darkened room, intoxicating those within it.

So it began, the plans, the hope, the duplicity and the betrayal. After some discussion this way and that, over who would lead the men from Derbyshire it was still not resolved. Robert Wain the chosen leader was now ill and could not march, so the committee looked for a replacement and Jeremiah's name mentioned.

They would march upon the ninth of June to make their world a better place. Having been told by other areas that they were ready, the London delegate himself claimed 70,000 would rise once they approached. Sir Francis Burdett himself waited upon this action, but they must secure Nottingham before any more could be done, it was to be a rallying point for the northern army that would come down to join them.

On Whit Monday, William Oliver the London delegate, attended the meeting at The Three Salmons, sending the compliments of Sir Francis Burdett when he called. Thomas Bacon trusted him unreservedly for he came with excellent recommendations, and gave a rousing address to lift the spirits of those who heard. Oliver, had been introduced among the Hampden clubs by Joseph Mitchell; a respected radical, from Lancashire; who advocated a vote for every man. He met Oliver in London with another leader of their movement, so he was accepted by all intent upon reform. Soon after however, Joseph Mitchell was arrested and imprisoned, unfortunately no one was to realise the connection.

Jeremiah was asked if he would attend a meeting the next day - the Tuesday, though he would have joined the enterprise there was never any doubt. To be assured they had the backing of the London radicals gave more substance to their cause. When Jeremiah was not certain on accepting leadership of the Derbyshire men. William Oliver told the room that if they did not rise they would be letting others areas down, who were far more fervent than they, to get the job done. Turning in an aside to those nearest. "I ask what man would leave his family and country so, when he could change all. *Stating that he had been round the circuit in Manchester, Yorkshire and was going to London by way of Birmingham. Every person was completely ready to rise and that he could raise 70,000 in London"* [1]

With many coming from the north and London behind them, this had to be the best opportunity to strike a blow for those suffering such hardship. It was not hard to believe, there were riots every now and then up and down the land. Though it was one thing being a Luddite with small attacks on machines in certain areas, quite another a countrywide rising. Jeremiah knew there were far greater risks in this, but watching his family sinking half-starved into despair with no way out drove him forward.

Leaving the meeting he decided not to tell Ann 'til it was truly necessary, for things so often went awry and he would have troubled her for nothing.

Both the Nottingham Committee and William Oliver considered Jeremiah the best replacement and he began to feel it was his duty. Persuaded by the warm congratulations of those who did not stand forward, though he would have joined the evening's work there was never doubt. Besides which he knew something no one else could know, that he had the courage and determination such a march would need. For the squalor of Nottingham left an imprint on his heart that only change could wash away.

———

However, a week or so later when the final plans were drawn together, Thomas Bacon, who'd spent thirty years agitating for this moment was not to join them. He was going to into hiding there was a warrant out for his arrest.

Jeremiah returned to Butchers Close knowing it was not the news Ann wanted, wondering if he could keep it from her, but the fact was he had no choice.

Walking down the filthy street he opened the door quietly, to find her stood like a disciple of the truth stood waiting for him.

The look upon his face told her something was to happen. "It is settled then?"

He stood, a moment. "I would like you to go home if I am away a while, you would have family around you then, to help with the children. I do not want you here alone."

Trying to smile, Ann still hoped it would be a way off yet. "When?"

Another silence, 'til he couldn't hold out any longer. "I will leave tomorrow."

She swallowed hard and studied him, there was something.

Jeremiah then stood very upright. "I will lead the men in Derbyshire."

The words swept the room leaving no sign of the devastation Ann felt. Holding her tears, she smiled. "I know it is right, that folk deserve much better than they get. You have promised to come back, and that is all I want, but I will look for you every moment you are gone from us."

"My beloved Ann, I promise and we will change this life."
Walking across the room to gather her into his arms, they sat a
while beside the fire, cradling each other making plans for the
future that was shining there before them; if only they could reach
it.

The next morning Jeremiah was up early and in good spirits, he
spent the morning playing with the children. Then as if it were a
normal day he strode across the room, to kiss Ann, "we will
change this life you will see." Then knelt upon the floor to kiss the
children. Smiling at them. "Look after your mother for me." Then
walked out of the door.

Ann stood a moment, after watching the door close.

Chapter Four

MR. HOLMES

There was to be a meeting in their room that evening, Alexander Amos gathered all the chairs he could, so those attending might sit to discuss matters, for which Ann was very grateful. If the children made a mess, she was quick to clean up. In ordinary times Ann would have busied herself making something to eat, all she could do now was keep the room tidy. It wasn't long before there was a tap on the door; wiping her hands upon her apron, and making sure her hair looked respectable in the cracked mirror that hung by the little window, not wanting to let Jeremiah down, she opened the door. Realising instantly who it was, a tall man with long scraggly hair reaching well below his shoulders stood in front of her. From what Jeremiah told her, he said little unless forced. Ann smiled. "Mr. Holmes?"

Narrow eyes searched her. "Yes lass."

In he came and there was something about him that made Ann warm to him; it wasn't long before they'd all arrived. Ann settled a bit out of the way, the children quite uninterested.

Then a more forceful knock, she sprang from her seat to see Henry Sampson stood beaming at her, inappropriate as always. Viewing him like she usually did, wanting to hold him away from her at the end of a very large stick. Knowing exactly what he'd say.

"Have I missed anything? Apologies for being late."

They settled themselves again, Sampson pushing between the wall and where Ann had been sat.

Holmes started up immediately. "You know my feelings and I will not discuss it now. I ask that we reconsider we need more information? Looking about the bare room, his eyes settling on the little boy playing with a wooden toy at Ann's feet, Elizabeth cuddling on her lap, taken with the coughing again, that was getting worse. "We should be certain about things, an' I don't mean by asking neither."

Instantly William Stevens the leader of the Nottingham Committee shot up, to stand as if on duty, looking with a sudden fury at John Holmes. "We made our decision, all of us, it is no different now."

Mr. Holmes got to his feet very slowly, cutting a very different figure to the one that walked in moments ago, towering over Stevens, jabbing his finger in his chest, "Well them that's certain, best be on the Forest, along wi' them that's ripe for it." Going to the door, then turning back. *"If I find any man is hunting my blood, I will hunt his."* [2] the door slamming behind him.

Stevens who appeared puce with rage seconds ago changed instantly, smiling indulgently at Ann, once Holmes was out of hearing, shaking his head. "Don't worry, Mr. Holmes is always a loose cannon."

The rest of the group nodded, and then proceeded as if Holmes had never spoken. This calmed Ann and she began to wonder whether Mr. Holmes was slightly unbalanced and her first appraisal wrong.

Stevens remained upon his feet and gave a lengthy speech. Time went on with Ann feeling tired again, a sense of disquiet reappearing.

The group were still discussing how many were to meet upon the Forest and the weapons they would have, their hope the Derbyshire men would keep to times set down. A jolly looking man Ann did not know burst into life. "Jeremiah knows what he must do."

Stevens had settled into his role remarking. "It is a matter of regret Robert Wain is not fit."

That was enough, though generally quiet Ann wasn't a woman that sat through being slighted. Smiling sweetly, she placed Elizabeth delicately to the floor and stood. "Well gentleman, I am certain Jeremiah will do his best. If you are willing to take that honour from him maybe he will not argue with you." Looking at Stevens with a smile that was about to freeze him. "Of course, I'm certain you gave good account of yourselves, that you may go in his stead before matters were concluded." Looking around, her eyes settling on Henry Sampson who started patting her arm much as you might placate a dog.

"Do not take on, 'tis only nerves we talk this way."

Ann flinched; there was something about him that did not sit so well with her.

The group looked from one to the other. "I think we will leave you be, we have taken up too much of your time already."

William Stevens smiling resignedly as if he'd said nothing wrong. "If you are in need of anything please get word to us by your neighbour."

All of them filing out, either nodding, or tipping their hat to her on leaving. Henry making a show of the fact he knew her beyond the meetings. Ann shut the door with some conviction, wondering what Jeremiah would say when he heard. She did not know then, that if she ever saw them again bar one, she would have liked to rip them limb from limb.

John Holmes's remarks began to rebound inside her head, almost as soon as they were gone. Ann tiptoed down the tiny passage to her neighbour to enquire exactly where he lived.

Alexander was sat within the doorway as if he'd been on watch. "I'm not sure where he lives lass, but I know where you will find him, he'll be in't Three Salmons at this time."

"If you are going, will you ask if he would talk to me?" Pleased she would be able to calm this doubt she felt.

"Aye, I'll ask."

Late afternoon the next day Ann heard Alexander come in and hurried through to see if he had any news. The answer was not what she'd expected. "He wasn't in't usual place. When I asked no one had seen him"

Nodding, she thanked him. "The Three Salmons is on the Market place?

Alexander had started to busy himself with some old blade, but turned back, coming through the doorway. "Aye it is, you're not going there are yu'?"

The question got no answer, Ann hurried off, to pluck Timothy from his playing and place a shawl around Elizabeth then hurried into the street.

On her return she fell exhausted in the chair beside the fire knowing nothing more than when she left. Only that Jeremiah would disapprove of her distressing herself, with the little ones to think of. The inn was full of rowdy men; it appeared all Nottingham knew something was up. Many knew Holmes, but no one had seen him. A few of the men tipped their hat to her, knowing who Jeremiah was; which heartened her, but did not stop the feeling that there was something she should know.

*

The day after Jeremiah left for Pentrich, on the sixth of June, the leaders of the northern armies were arrested at a meeting near Dewsbury and imprisoned. Suspicion was mounting against William Oliver, the London delegate; John Holmes did not know this when he'd attended the meeting at Butchers Close. The mere fact William Oliver travelled inside a carriage, that was far more money than most could afford, added to the way he dressed, was more than enough for John Holmes to think him a fraud.

Threatening Oliver openly at another meeting on the seventh and only Stevens, the leader of the Nottingham committee, with his constant backing of him was to stop John Holmes from giving Oliver the ending he deserved. Very nearly unmasked for the duplicitous liar that he was; but Oliver knew how to turn things, being quick with his tongue like the rich establishment he served and managed to deflect suspicion.

Unfortunately for Jeremiah having left early on the fifth, he and the marchers of Pentrich and South Wingfield were not to know of these arrests and no one saw fit to tell them.

Chapter Five

THEM THAT DARES

After walking the seventeen miles to Pentrich, Jeremiah could not help but think it was just a few miles from Sutton and hoped his wife and children were now there. Both he and Thomas Bacon went inside The White Horse, which was to be their meeting place. Jeremiah turned off and went to sit against to the back wall.

Thomas Bacon was a stout old man with white hair, a black hat and long coat, with skin the texture of porridge. A group quickly surrounded him, the landlady who happened to be his sister shouting to him. "Now then Tom?"

He turned to find no one behind him and looked perplexed, then saw Jeremiah sitting nonchalantly against the wall.

The group searched the room for one they thought fitting, their eyes settling on Jeremiah, eyebrows raised, looking back at Thomas Bacon.

Jeremiah sat quietly; when they'd settled to the idea he raised his hat and continued to sit and watch. He was around five foot six in height with a dark complexion and curling brown black hair. When he spoke there was something about him that set him apart. Carrying a courage and determination to see through most things and though he did not play to it, women always looked on him with a great deal of interest.

After half an hour a tall young man walked purposefully across the room offering his hand, smiling broadly. "George, George

Weightman, I am pleased to meet you Captain. I'll get a drink, you must be ready for it. I'm told you've walked from Nottingham?"

Jeremiah lifted his hat. "Aye. I would not expect it of you."

With the last remnants of a smile George turned off. "It'll be my honour Sir, the landlady is my mother so you need not worry over it."

"Thank ye then, I'll not say no." Within ten minutes Jeremiah was eating an enormous plate of stew to go with the ale.

The others in the group waited until he'd finished before approaching. Pushing the plate to one side, another tall man, older than Jeremiah walked over.

"William Turner, Captain; I hear you served your country at one time?"

Jeremiah nodded. "About five years, 'til I tired of it and left at a time of my choosing." Smiling sardonically.

Truth was William Turner could not see why they needed someone no one knew coming to take over the small army they'd assembled. It was even more of a slight when this man was small in stature, and had the look of a Romani to boot. Turner pulled up a chair. "Have you a plan of action Captain?"

The Nottingham Captain seemed to know his mind.

" You have served yourself I'm told?"

"I have seen action in many places, that is true Captain."

Jeremiah nodded. "Then I will have great need of your experience, are there others that have served within the ranks?"

"Not that I know of."

"Then we need to put some order within the men before we set out."

Thomas Bacon came across with the rest of the group and soon the table was surrounded, the talk going on into the evening.

It was a night Jeremiah's heart was set upon its course, telling all who listened that it mattered little if those in opposition heard, they would be washed away with a tide that would sweep all before it, when the northern armies descended upon Nottingham. If he had doubts whether they would accept him, that night they were answered.

The next day after a walk over the area and from what he'd seen upon the journey there, he knew it would not be easy. With so much ground to cover, and having to call at different houses to commandeer their weapons or men, he realised his force may have to split to save the time to do this. Talking at length with William Turner and George Weightman, who seemed to him to be true of character and very set upon this venture.

That night in the White Horse while they went over the plan, an older man came through the gathering to stand before him.

"Isaac Ludlam, Captain." A small group following: instantly Jeremiah caught the look of pride worn by those who pushed the elder man forward. He rose from his seat remembering William Turner had mentioned the name and the work that had gone into preparing the weapons Isaac had hidden in Coburn quarry.

Jeremiah stood and shook his hand. "Sit with us Isaac, William's told me of the work that's gone into preparing for this venture. I can only thank you most sincerely for it." The group spread out behind him, one lad laid a hand upon his father's shoulder in support, when he sat down. "I will need men to keep order in our army and I would ask this of you Isaac if you would take it?"

Isaac Ludlam looked slightly surprised; the hand upon his shoulder pressed him on. "Well Captain I would be proud to accept." He smiled. The group in support of Isaac appeared to have grown and there was a general nodding of approval going on. William Turner and George Weightman looked at each other, acknowledging the right of this decision.

Isaac Ludlam was a Methodist preacher and his word swayed many in the village, for he was of a sound character and if ever help were needed, he was the man many sought.

The following day passed with drills and much village interest, the lifting of hats and eyes assessing this young stranger. The day wore on, and the way he held himself provoked a very different opinion to the one first held by the look of his attire. Numbers had grown and the men seemed to have no doubts about their Captain now. However, when he spoke hearts swelled and a firmness of purpose was produced, there could be no other course.

Jeremiah was charismatic and able to assess a man quickly; with the radicals in London backing them, he earnestly believed this to be the way forward. How could he not, having watched his own family deprived of hope and half-starved into the bargain. How could he not believe there were those all over the country just as he, ready to rise and overthrow this oppressive uncaring government that transported men for poaching, or hung a boy for burning a hayrick. That let folk lie out in the street and starve rather than control the merchants' greed and give men a proper wage for the work they did. He had worked upon a song for them to march to and handed out sheets of paper with it on.

> Every man his skill must try,
> He must turn out and not deny;
> No bloody soldier must he dread,
> He must turn out and fight for bread;
> The time has come you plainly see,
> The government opposed must be.

Remembering the songs sung while with the twenty-eighth, it had been one of the best things about it. Though he missed the laughter of friends, he also remembered having to stand against his own, something that did not sit so well with him.

He'd warmed to William Turner knowing he had seen heavy service for his country. William was tall and strong; he was also very intent upon their purpose, having attended meetings with Thomas Bacon well before the rising was a reality.

In deserting, William Turner knew Brandreth was far from alone, many left the ranks at a time of their own choosing it was common at the time.

The days were now about drills and the nights were spent in

The White Horse, sat at the table going over and over the plan, showing every man the map in his possession. The marks upon it showing the different areas that would to rise with them.

On the day of the ninth he was living on adrenaline wishing away the hours till it was time to set out for a better day. In truth he'd not thought of Ann or the children since he arrived, he had, had so much to do, but right at this moment they were all he thought of. The hopes of this venture were to free them from the poverty they endured and those like them. He stood remembering what it was to touch Ann's hair, to take Lizzie into his arms and swing her round, ruffle Timothy's mop of curls until he burst out laughing at the faces he pulled. Just for that moment he wanted nothing more than to walk straight back to Nottingham take Ann in his arms and have the children round him, forget this march and everything else, but nothing then would change. He also remembered what it was to hear them cry themselves to sleep; when there was no food to be had, and that same anger swelled inside. Instead of going home he stood by Hunts Barn in the rain, many already gathered.

"Captain, we are ready." William Turner stood to attention.

"Indeed. It was then the 'Nottingham Captain' gave the order." Looking one to the other with a quiet smile.

The small army formed into a line two abreast and marched out of the village, some never to see it again, stopping to collect the weapons Isaac Ludlam had hidden in the Quarry.

Then on to Wingfield Park, things going much slower than

anticipated, and to add to that a few wanted to "Draw the badger." A term used for settling the score with Colonel Wingfield Halton, for the unfortunate four that were to hang for burning his hayricks, wanting to draw him from his property and shoot him.

Jeremiah remembered telling Ann about it before he left, considering they could administer justice when all was secure in the country. Stopping only at houses marked out for holding weapons and men suitable for action. At one the householder offered a gun and nothing more, Jeremiah was quite sure they had more and struck the man, at which William Turner laid hold of him, not wanting to use the man ill. There was no aggression in it, but Jeremiah feared their resolve, for they must be ready for what this night might hold. No rising throughout history was ever won without a battle. The Captain shoved past him without a word, grabbing a candle from the table, lighting it at the fire before going upstairs, the old man started to remonstrate with him again, but Jeremiah was not of a mind to listen. Pointing with his eyes, "You." at William and one of Isaac Ludlam's sons, "With me," up they went to bring down a lad and another gun. The lad was unwilling but had little option, and so was pressed forward.

On they marched, to Buckland Hollow where one woman was proving particularly obstinate refusing to open the door, there was a great deal of shouting. Jeremiah went alone to the back of the house demanding entrance there was a shot when he forced open the shutters. Old guns were not always secure; the silence broken by the sound of crying, others came. He heard voices from inside. "Is he dead?"

Speaking with those he trusted away from other ears to ascertain who it was and whether they were dead or not, Jeremiah felt himself drain of colour. None too happy to learn the man was either dead or close to it, they walked on Jeremiah becoming firmer in his actions. Unsure if he had dealt the blow, the man in all likelihood was getting ready to join their ranks. He had to put it from his mind if they were to get to Nottingham, and if the night went the way they planned, it would not be the last blood spilt, though not what he had wanted.

On meeting the group from Pentrich he was to learn they had not commandeered anyone at all, or any weapons. It was all still to be done, causing delay and lost time, so decided to split their forces, Isaac Ludlam, William Turner and himself one way, Edward Turner and George Weightman the other, meeting again once they'd gone through the village.

Jeremiah had expected their numbers to strengthen; they had, but not to the extent anticipated. Sending George Weightman into a yard they passed to get a pony to ride on ahead to Nottingham and see how it went there. Watching him disappear into the distance, hoping for good news on his return.

They were approaching the Iron works at Butterley, the march going far too slowly, they could not afford to stop there now. Wanting to keep to his orders from the committee and time was not upon their side.

On seeing men he knew George Goodwin, the manager of the Iron works, was soon out amongst them hoping to cajole them into returning home, telling all who listened they would hang. Jeremiah did not want a recurrence of earlier events, noting the presence of a number of Special Constables, after telling Goodwin he wanted his men.

Goodwin turned and stood squarely before him, *"You are going with halters about your necks and will all be hanged."[3]*

The Captain scanned him a moment, considering him to be much braver than many in coming out to remonstrate with them. Deciding then to turn off, he hadn't the time, they were already behind schedule and in a loud clear voice shouted his orders "March on." Wondering how they knew to have extra protection, but then they had not been particularly secretive at The White Horse? Thinking about the lads that had listened to their plans, who openly said they'd enlisted as Special Constables that day. Laughing, saying they'd done it for the money they received on signing up. How else did they know extra Constables might be needed? The thought niggled away; making him glad he'd sent George Weightman on ahead. It would, however, be a very small matter when the thousands that were expected, began to converge upon Nottingham.

It was raining heavily and some of his army started to slip away into the night. The shooting and the manager of the Ironworks had unsettled them, and the numbers they expected were not coming forward they'd been told to expect.

Isaac Ludlam and his sons, however, were keeping good order at the back of the line, which offered Jeremiah some small measure of relief.

They got to Codnor and the rain was coming with a passion, they were in need of some refreshment, calling at different inns along the way, telling the landlord the bill would be paid in time.

Marching on George Weightman reappeared; a crowd surrounding him immediately listening to what he had to say. The Captain drew him to one side, the rain still hammering down and did not seem to want to stop.

George had the best of news; Nottingham was taken and the troops would not come from the barracks. There was a lightening of mood; a few considered it so good there would be little need for them. It took some persuasion to get them moving again. Reaching The Junction Navigation Inn at Langley Mill, one of his army had been shot after a gun went off by accident and a doctor was called, so the man was left behind. Although the doctor fearing for his safety came to the conclusion he wasn't needed after all and left.

At the Sun Inn at Eastwood, a different picture emerged villagers came over in a state of panic, all saying the same thing. A magistrate had been through and was heading for the barracks to raise the soldiers and deal with any revolt and more of his army slipped away into the night. One man turned off in full view cursing; the Captain watched, his men waited to see what was to happen, he had little choice but try and stop him. *"If you do not fall into line I will put a bullet in you."*

At this the deserter walked back to face him, suddenly bringing out a knife, he thrust it at his Captain. *"Shove that gun at me, an' I will hack your head off."* Sneering, he turned, showing Jeremiah his back, leaving him little choice but level the gun at the now retreating figure, he must stop him or many would soon follow. *"Get back in line now or I will put a bullet in you."* [4]

There was no answer, the Captain had no choice if he was to keep this army together, leveling the gun he fired, at that moment a hand shot out from the line of men beside him, to throw his aim and the bullet sailed into the scrub beyond.

Jeremiah looked at the deserter's saviour; Thomas Turner had begun to sweat profusely and looked away. The Captain studied him, then gave the order, "march on" leaving the absconder to his own devices.

Jeremiah had a force of about two hundred, at some points some said four hundred, a number having caught up with them just past Eastwood. However, the doubts were not to be dismissed and he was now concerned with what or who had managed to get the magistrate out. If Nottingham was taken, had news of that stimulated him into action, highly unlikely, he came from the opposite direction. Maybe the manager of Butterly Ironworks had sent word to him. Half smiling, the magistrate would get a surprise when he arrived in Nottingham, if the news George Weightman came with was correct and settled his mind to his orders, they were already so far behind schedule.

Marching on, the rain trickling down the back of his neck, he wondered how many would meet them on the Forest. Would they have gone into Nottingham already? If Nottingham were already taken, there'd not be much to do. They were nearing the Gilt brook a stream between Eastwood and Kimberly still a number of miles from their destination, when the cry went up. *"Run, Miles soldiers!"* [5] At least twenty Dragoons, still half a mile off, sabres drawn, but half a mile is soon gained with a horse beneath you.

The effect was immediate, many cast their weapons aside and fled, Jeremiah stood firm yelling out commands. "Stand, form a line and hold." A small line formed, William Turner thundering orders. "Stand and hold." William looked towards his Captain.

Jeremiah stood fast, William beside him. "Stand and hold." Again, a small line formed. Those left realised they were lost without the need for words, the few that formed a line looked to each other, then decided on their best course so many had already gone and the action decided was not to stand and fight. So many had cast their weapons to one side. William Turner and his Captain shared another glance, there was no choice now but to flee. William followed the disappearing army, jumping over different weapons that were strewn across the ground in all directions.

Jeremiah had enough presence of mind to head south, seeing most racing back the way they'd come. Surely that would be the first place the soldiers would expect them to go. How could this have happened if Nottingham were taken, Jeremiah's mind was in turmoil? Heading away from where he thought the soldiers would expect him. Yet there was only one place he wanted to be now, by the fire with Ann and the little ones, sat against it, hoping the hunger pangs inside his stomach would abate, for lean times were even leaner times for him. He ran and ran until he could not hear a sound, keeping off the track and close to the undergrowth. If the slightest movement occurred, he went straight for the bushes.

Listening, hoping not to hear the sound of pikes being swept across the hedgerow searching him out. Nothing, just silence, even that was terrifying, a heavy rustling and a badger came into view then another, disappearing quickly, he must have disturbed them. His thoughts bitter, wishing he'd not stopped his fallen army when they wanted to "Draw the Badger" at least they would have achieved something that night. At least they'd be avenged for the four that were to hang for doing nothing more than fire a couple of hayricks. He'd heard from the men that they were barely twenty. Then the awful futility of it hit, that they would to lose their lives for that. Another bitterness, if Nottingham was taken had his force been the only one to fail.

Yet if Nottingham was taken, where did the soldiers come from? The news George had been given could not have been correct. Sinking into the undergrowth, his thoughts cutting him in two, hoping against hope his small army could elude the Dragoons long enough to get away. Realising when he thought of Ann, that he would not see her again in triumph as he had dared to hope.

Indeed, the reality was that he was unlikely to ever see her again. The tears he tried to hold coursed his face; the children he loved so dearly; he would never see grow. He must leave England and maybe one day he might send for them. This was the only thought that gave him consolation now. Then remembering the money he had been given to join the march, if he could keep that he had a chance, each man having paid.

It stopped raining quite suddenly, he lay huddled in the undergrowth, the sun shining now like nothing was amiss. The undergrowth before him glistening from the night's rain, his clothes soaked, he must keep moving, unsure which route to take, he raised himself. Having marched through the night he now wanted to put as much distance behind him and those pursing him as he could. Keeping to the hedgerows, until coming to the point where the Derwent meets the Trent. Waiting 'til he felt it was safe to get across, he was wet enough already and did not want to swim. There were too many folk about now for his liking, after getting across he decided it would be better to hide out 'til evening and move on then.

Evening came and hunger followed, not having eaten, but it was something he was used to, moving quickly when the light was strong enough to show the way. Good fortune came to his aid, just when he was about to leave the track, a rabbit lay before him, its throat torn out. A weasel or stoat maybe, they had the strongest jaws for size of any animal he knew, surely it would have carried this prize off, no matter now, he was the lucky recipient. Though it would have to be very late indeed for it to be dark enough to hide the smoke from such a fire. Picking his way between the trees, until hidden by them, he felt inside his pocket for the berries he'd collected, popping them one at a time into his mouth. It was like nectar, some were tart but he couldn't afford to be picky.

Thinking about Ann, tonight it looked like he would dine better than his wife, looking at the rabbit, wishing with all his heart he could send some back to Nottingham. Peeling the skin back, the purple red of the meat shining back. Remembering with an ironic smile it was a smell when cooking he hated with a passion, Rabbit had a sickly sweet smell, so distinct from everything else. He'd gotten used to it by now, hunger managed to cure all sorts of passions at one swipe. It wasn't going to bother him tonight either. Remembering then that Ann would be in Sutton, so his family would be looked after there well enough. He had no worries on that score and settled his mind about it.

Days began to blend into one another; he had no more good fortune, and resigned himself to plundering someone's chickens when the opportunity arose. Moving close to any farms he passed, not having eaten anything at all for a good few days. Then as if by magic strutting through the hedge in and out of the field just in front of him, any number of chickens. Looking about him, feeling more the fool than hunter trying to catch one, he fell. Getting to his knees it appeared that he'd caught something after all, breaking its neck when he went down. This would keep him fed a couple of days, stuffing it into the pocket of the brown greatcoat, and moving quickly from the scene, another offence to add onto a growing list.

*

Before Jeremiah left Nottingham they had agreed between them, that Ann should take the coach home well before the ninth. Having sold some of the tools he used for mending the knitting frames, to get the money together for her journey.

Staying later than agreed was a decision Ann would regret, but there was little choice; Lizzie's chest was worse than it had ever been, making her cough enough to retch, like her grandfather. The damp room in which they lived having done nothing to help.

On the night of the ninth Ann went up into the market place to get a remedy from one of the so-called Doctor's who lived upon the corner and saw exactly what was happening. Using some of the money Jeremiah had given her for the coach to do it. Crowds of men stood in groups small and large, some were singing the old Luddite songs on the far side of the market square and her heart began to swell with hope and pride.

Hurrying back to tell Mrs. Amos what was taking place and thank her for watching the children. There were many ways to gain money in these hard times, settling herself to stay in their little room, considering it would be the safest when the marchers came. Foregoing the pleasure of watching her husband stride into Nottingham a hero and if there was to be any looting, no one would be coming to Butchers Close to do it.

Sitting on the broken chair most of the night to hear nothing,

86

while trying to get Lizzie to swallow her medicine, which she didn't want to take, neither was it working. Listening to the steady flow of folk back to their homes, to fall asleep in the chair when most were upon the business of the day.

It was later that afternoon when Mrs. Amos came all of a sweat, a look of horror on her face. Crouching beside Ann who sat immobile, hurriedly telling her that they were routed.

Ann picked up Timothy, wrapped a shawl round Lizzie, and made her way up past the Red Lion to turn on Hollow Stone. Only to see a wagon coming through with a weary set of men all roped together, the Dragoons beside it looking very pleased with themselves. Her heart sinking beyond anything she'd felt before; at least Jeremiah wasn't there. Sickened by the sight, her mind fought with every the possibility, was he already dead, how would she know, there was no one she could ask? Suddenly having to stop and retch in a side street, the children clinging to her. This hideous scene playing over and over inside her head, once back inside their little room she stood not sure what she should do, her mind flying from one thing to the other. Considering she had no other course but leave, how could she, Lizzie wasn't well enough to make the journey?

Hurrying to her neighbour to tell her what she'd seen and ask if she would take the children to her father if anything should happen and he would see her right.

"Aye lass if it comes to that." The older woman close to tears hugged her like she didn't want to let her go. Holding each arm she looked earnestly into her face. "You should go now, it's what Jerry would want. He won't come here; he thinks you left for Sutton days ago and if he does, I'll tell him you are off home."

Ann walked back into their room, Mrs. Amos following, then turned again in panic, "But Lizzie isn't well?" In so much distress she wasn't thinking properly.

The older woman smiled. "The fresh air will be better for her than these damp walls, wrap the blanket round her. Gather yourself a minute then be off, you need to get them children away from here, I'll get something for you." Coming back with a bowl of broth. "I doubt you've eaten last few days," placing the bowl on the floor beside the fire."

Almost falling on the chair Ann grabbed her hand and kissed it. "You're a good friend, an there's not so many when times turn."

Mrs. Amos smiled and sat beside her a while 'til Ann was more herself and thinking rationally, then left not wanting to disturb the children.

Timothy had settled, while Lizzie sat upright beside him dozing, then coughing every now and then, Ann leant across to pull the blankets round her. Mrs. Amos always had a presence that calmed them and it was no different now. She sat gazing at the grate, should she rebuild the fire, one small area aglow, surrounded by a ring of ash a reminder of their dreams.

With no sound or any warning, the door burst open with a force that took it from its hinges, special constables raced into the room throwing everything about. Hurtling from the bed Lizzie hid behind her mother's skirt while Ann grabbed a hold of Timothy. Before the constables threw off the mattress, to find an old rusty blade without a handle that wasn't good for anything. Knowing who she was, one took a firm hold of her arm leering at her, only letting go when Lizzie screamed, then coughed so much Ann thought her lungs would burst. Leaving as quickly as they came, to go straight to Alexander's, she heard them throwing furniture, angered perhaps having found nothing of use to them.

Knowing they were supporters of the cause could only mean someone had informed upon them, how else would they know exactly who was involved in the battle for reform and where they lived. Nothing would ever be the same, but if they were still looking for Jeremiah at least he had evaded them so far and in that way Ann felt a surge of hope and a defiant pride.

However, the stark reality was that she was never likely to see him again. Maybe he would head for America though he had little money. Hurriedly gathering what meagre bits they had, looking at the children, knowing they would need to be carried most of the way. Putting her hand into the pocket of her skirt Ann found the money Jeremiah had given her and wanted so to cry, she could get the coach after all. Creeping past Alexander's, to find no one in the little room, had the soldiers taken them her thoughts all over the place?

Hurrying up the alley toward Fisher gate, the little gutter running with blood from the folk who plied their trade there. Walking as quickly as she could, afraid to run for fear it drew someone's attention. Knowing at any moment the soldiers could reappear from another home they'd ransacked and decide to take her after all. Avoiding Hollow Stone and the gaol, past the graveyard to Goose Gate and Broad Street, once past St. Mary's workhouse, no one would know who she was anyway. Relieved when a coach came to a halt beside her, struggling with the children and her clothing to offer him her money all that she had.

Taking a cursory look, a rasping voice dismissed her. "You'll need more than that today, out the way, there's proper folk here waiting.'

Ann grabbed a hold of Lizzie who was being pulled from her when those 'proper folk' pushed past. Spilling what was left of the coins into the dirt, struggling to pick it up while holding Timothy, until the coach set off to leave her choking in a cloud of dust. Lizzie fighting to breathe, which seemed to go so very shallow. Ann fearing she might leave for a better place right there and then. If ever there was a time to cry it would be now, instead she must go on, the money could be put to better use inside her pocket after all. Once past St. Mary's workhouse, no one would recognise her anyway, that would be one less worry.

Hurrying along relieved to get on the road to Sutton, to watch another coach go rattling past, only to disappear into the distance. Looking at the windmills near the caves, not likely to ever see inside them now, should she take refuge there, from what she'd been told some did, her mind flitting from one thing to the other. Considering it best to head for Sutton not knowing who might be inside them. Even if the soldiers came for her once she was home, at least the children would be safe.

The journey home was fifteen miles and the children did not want to walk; she was having to carrying them then rest, so it was going to take a while. Timothy's crying started up almost as soon as the journey. Ann tried to think of happier times and hold onto the hope Jeremiah could elude the authorities long enough to get away. Sinking onto a bit of grass to rest again beside muddy, well rutted track, a cart rattling past until it slowed, the driver turning to shout over his shoulder. "Where thee off Miss, I'm on't way t'other side a Hucknall if it's any help to thee?"

Ann could not get to her feet fast enough. "That would be a great help, that is if you do not mind a crying child." Trying desperately to hush Timothy.

The young man smiled. "Tis no trouble, I'm glad t' help thee." Jumping from the cart to hold Timothy who hushed his crying instantly on finding a stranger holding him, helping Ann up, while she'd manhandled Lizzie up onto the seat.

"An' do not worry 'bout the crying, I am more than used t' that." Smiling at her while giving Timothy a cheeky grin that seemed to stun him into a further silence, placing him back into Ann's care once she was up onto the seat. Jumping up to sit at the opposite end, the children squashed into the middle.

The young man's chatter lasted throughout the journey and Ann was very glad of it, taking her mind from other matters. Finally helping her down a good way past Hucknall. "I'd take thee all the way Miss, but it'll make me late, an' I cannot afford to lose the work."

"You have been more than kind. Thank you." Offering him the coins within her pocket.

"He smiled. Save tha' money for t' children," setting off at a rattling pace, waving a goodbye, urging the old horse onwards again."

Thankfully the day was warm but Ann was still anxious over Lizzie who seemed unusually tired, but wasn't coughing quite so much, the sun having shone enough to cheer those without her worries. Thinking over their last night together, how could she have been stupid enough to let him go? If she had told him she thought she was pregnant again and was feeling pain, he would have stayed. It was the perfect excuse, but no, they were both much too naïve for their own good. Now her mind fought with every possibility, was Jeremiah already dead? Trying to turn her mind from it, only for another recollection to burst forth. Walking through the door at Bedlam Court after seeing Jeremiah every day since they first meet, her father sat by the fire wearing an expression like the vicar, when he was to give a sermon.

"Now lass, sit thee sen' down." Unable to avoid him she sat on the little stool Hannah wasn't using at the moment, watching drifts of smoke disappear into the soot stained chimney back, like secrets from another time.

"This lad tha's seein'." Waiting for her reaction, when there was none, he'd started up again. "He's gunna ger his sen in trouble an' no mistake." Still nothing.

George however had an inkling the smoke coming wouldn't be going up the chimney. "Lass, he seems all rate what I've seen on him, but I'm your father, an' I want you safe. An' from what I hear he's a bit tougher than he lets on." He'd paused. "I hear things. The' talk down t' pit tha' knows."

Ann had stopped him there, well past simmering. "What is it you've heard? We had this talk when I met Jeremiah and nothing's changed. You want me to marry the Sedgwick lad who sits behind his father's counter hiding from life?"

George put his hand to his forehead, the idea not without some merit. Trying again. "Look lass I want what's best for thee. He'll end on't gallows if he dun't changes his ways." The moment it came out of his mouth, he'd regretted it.

"What is it you've heard, for goodness sake. There's been half the town a Ludding at some time." Looking exasperatedly at him.

"Aye but thee not walkin' out wi' my daughter are thee?" It was the first time she'd seen her father anywhere close to angry.

Sprinting from the room, shouting back at him. "Well if he does, I'll be beside him if he'll have me, and you can sit in the bloomin' shop."

George had closed his eyes; he had an idea the conversation would end that way. At least now he knew her heart lay with this highly principled young man and there was nothing he could do to change it, turning to look back into the fire.

Ann remembered running to her room, arguing with her sisters, never having dared speak to her father like that before.

George though was not the type that set draconian rules for his children, knowing it would only force her away and that was the last thing he wanted.

The memories receded and eventually Ann had sight of home, and wondered what her reception would be.

Someone must have alerted them, for next minute she saw Bill Rowbotham racing down Back Lane, her heart leaping at the sight, her father there beside him. Bill was soon taking the children one in each arm, while her father lifted her from her feet to carry her across his arms back to the house she was so very glad to see.

For a while no one spoke, just low voices and everyone scurrying around to get them comfortable as quickly as they could. A hot drink was pushed into her hands while her mother tended to the youngsters, who could be heard laughing, then coughing. Their laughter giving Ann a sense of relief she hadn't felt for quite a while, wishing Jeremiah was beside her to share it. After an hour or so George followed her up to bed, then sat at the bottom of it saying naught, just waiting for her to tell him all.

"I'm sorry to have to come."

Stopping her immediately, he smiled. "Hey lass tha' dun't need t' tell me tha's sorry for comin' here."

Ann gazed at him unable to express her love, and the relief that flooded her body now. "A cart stopped for us, I don't know what time I'd have got here if he hadn't, the children were not for walking. "

George gave a deep sigh. "Thank the lord someone stopped for thee. An' I dun't care what folk say, today or any other. Over t' years I got to know that lad a' thine and I'm proud to know him, so, there's no need to apologise t' me. Truth is, it's I that should do that."

It wasn't the reaction Ann expected.

George was sitting very upright now at the end of the bed. "I said things I shun't 'ah."

Ann knew exactly what he meant.

"That lad can't help him sen no more than you could falling for him. Some are different, a bit stronger, an' you can't all is see it straight away. He's done what he considered rate, an' that's what all on us should do. Only most are too afraid, an' hide behind a load a bluster." George looked at his daughter, pride shining through the pain. "An' that's what makes a man that's more than t'others, them that dares. Does tha' know any a what happened?"

Ann shook her head.

"It'll be hard to hear lass, but I dun't want anyone else tellin' thee." He stopped to gather himself. "Afore yu' come, Rueben were here, he's got someone on't coaches that passes messages tha' knows. Tellin' us there'd been a march, an' Dragoons come, wi' Jeremiah an' another, a William Turner, trying to hold 'um. Saying them that marched thought country were rising, but word had gone through that northern leaders were arrested, so not so many turned out. Day or two afore yesterday they were arrested, is what Rueben said. The were a meeting on't seventh in Nottingham, an' one at committee, a man named Holmes confronted this London delegate, sayin' he were a bloody informer, but most a t'others stuck by him, saying all should go on, for London were ready. This Holmes chap were going do for him, a man called Oliver."

Ann sat bolt upright unable to breathe, knowing now what John Holmes had tried to do.

George saw the pain this news had caused, took a moment and ploughed on. "Bill came round just afore yu' come, thought you'd be comin' that's when we went to look for thee. He said there'd been some unrest in Huddersfield an' a few other places, but leaders were in prison, so it come to naught, just arrested as many poor buggers as the' could. Said market place at Nottingham were swelled, waiting for Derby lot to come, there were a bit of a ruckus there but it come to nought."

Ann saw her father close to tears, not daring to tell him she had seen this for herself, learning to her horror how their bravery had come to naught.

"So lass, thy lad turns out to be bravest of lot on um, an' them from Derbyshire. Though it in't goin' to help um any, or thee in't long run. If he needs help an' I can give it. If we knew where he were it had be a start?" Looking earnestly at her.

Ann shook her head. "I don't know. They'll be no one he trusts now. But he won't know will he, that no one else marched? I can't believe they would do that. They knew things were turning

———

on the seventh, if they had doubt. They had two days to warn them, they have hung them in the open for carrion to pick at, why?" Too distressed to feel anything other than a pained confusion.

"I only know what's gerrin through. You rest lass; them children need yu." Turning from her, "I'll leave you be, your mothers happy as a singin' kettle you're here, where tha' belongs, an' them children. We can hope most are hiding out, along wi' our lad eh', till they can get to other lands, or it all goes quiet, one at t'other." He smiled. "If the' catch him, when he comes out there'll be a place here tha' knows, so don't be worrying 'bout that. An I dun't care what folk say or think, or ruddy overseer either." However, George Bridget was certain, if they caught Jeremiah, he would not be coming home, he was trying to cheer his daughter into believing it might be. Remembering very clearly, supposing Ann did also, the time he'd warned of just such an event.

Heartened as she was to have her family's support, it was the bitterest news to hear the rising Jeremiah believed he was a part of, had been all but stopped up north two days before he marched. Leaving their efforts without a hope, so why in God's name had no one warned them? Surely he would not risk his life on such a basis, or those with him? Though desperate for change, he must have believed others were to join them, there had to be more than one informer to bring all this about. A rising that would have gone ahead at some point, to what effect who knows. Little realising then the government had actively encouraged it, so they could put the fear of God into a starving, restless populace.

*

In the days that followed Ann's worries were ever present, but she was now more fortunate than those in Derbyshire, after a search of Bedlam Court, the authorities had taken to watching the surrounding streets and left them well alone. News filtered through daily, however, of more arrests, all sent straight to gaol, Jeremiah's name never among them.

The villager's of Pentrich and South Wingfield were under watch, men searched constantly for the remaining marchers and made life unbearable for those left behind. The starving and desperate it seemed must accept the situation, and doff their caps at those with money enough not to care. Trotting out the same dire remarks to compensate for a lack of moral compass. Or walking briskly by some huddled pauper with nowhere left to go.

Chapter Six

LOVE BEYOND PRICE

Jeremiah's clothes were splattered with mud, if he were to avoid capture, he'd need to look better than he did. Going down to the brook at the bottom of the incline, drinking first, then rubbing at the dirt upon his clothes. In the end he took them off to rub vigorously at them. Then laid them out upon a sunlit mossy bank that stood deep within this woodland, having washed, and feeling much better for it.

The day's fell into one another, he had no knowledge where he was or even when he'd last eaten. All he knew was he needed to get to Brighton he had a sister there, hoping she might help him. Praying word about the rising had not travelled that far south, though he knew that hope might be a faint one.

Thinking back to the day they caused havoc at Betts Frames, throwing everything into the street, the noise ringing across town. There had been at least a thousand men that night; when a small mounted cavalry detachment appeared scattering them.

Some of the lads went off in the direction of South Normanton knowing more machines needed breaking there. In hindsight there wasn't much difference between that night and his small force. In reality how could he hope with a few hundred men that they could resist a mounted detachment with rifles and swords, bearing down on them at speed? This heartened him, though he knew history might portray them harshly. Any that did he mused, he would like to see make a stand of their own in such a circumstance. The flapping mouth is always open and from what he knew, the first to run. He remembered watching the old women hissing at the cavalry, children throwing the broken frames that lay about, and the cavalry not knowing where to turn. Alf and Bill trying not to laugh, watching them ride up and down Back Lane to Smedley's End, not sure which way to go.

Recalling another attack where he'd gone through a skylight in the attic, gently putting the window down after him. To hear them climb the stairs his heart thumping, while he crept across the roof to get behind the chimneystack, going back the same way when they'd left.

Another where two soldiers were stationed inside a house to protect the frames from any Ludd's daft enough to attempt an attack. Leaving their weapons propped up at the back wall. Alf had nodded to him when the door opened, considering they could grab their weapons, for the soldiers could do naught without them. There were six Ludd's, including Jeremiah and it gave him an instant lift to think of it now. Bursting in to take the weapons, rendering the soldiers useless, two Ludd's stood guard over them, another couple at the door, while they took in 'Enoch', the large hammer that was used to do the damage. Racing off after with the rifles, a prize in all honesty they were never likely to use. When word went round what they had done, they were the toast of many a night, no one sure exactly who they were toasting, which suited them.

He had been in many scrapes before evading the government, only now they would know his name and all about him. They'd hardly been secretive at The White Horse, a huge mistake in hindsight. Wondering if it had been the two newly recruited constables that spent the night in their company who'd alerted the magistrate.

Though his heart desired it, he knew he must keep well away from where he'd like to be. Hoping Ann would have the forethought to distance herself and in that way protect herself and the children. They had not talked of such an outcome, now he saw clearly that he should have. What worried him the most was that Ann if anything was as staunch a support as a man could hope for, which was not what he wanted from her now. It was a constant worry to him now that this might bring her trouble.

Though Ann's father was an easygoing man, Jeremiah was certain he would not stand for anyone threatening his family. While the men who worked the mines were not slow to help those they viewed as close as kin, so tried to settle his mind about it.

His thoughts going back to the huge Luddite attack, many coming from Bulwell, Arnold and Basford, all meeting at the seven mile stone. It was the night he met Henry Sampson, who was to become a close friend, recalling how he'd saved his neck that night, pulling him down a hidden *jennel, when the soldiers were closing in. Risking his life to do it, for he was already out of sight.

As leader of this rising, there was little hope of compassion, but the reality was it had been a riot nothing more. They'd never even been read the riot act, so in law should be allowed back to their families, except for the shooting of Robert Walters.

He pondered if he'd have been best going to Henry for help in the first place, but he'd travelled so far south now the idea wasn't viable.

Having stayed within this woodland far too long already he shook himself from such considerations, his clothes looking so much better for being washed. If he were to get a meal inside him, this had to be the time to do it. The greatcoat looked cleaner and with luck he might sell it. Moving his money into his jacket pocket and separating what he needed for a meal. Not wanting anyone to know how much he had, for thieves were everywhere and he could not replace it.

It was still light when he went towards an inn that didn't seem to have that many houses near, walking quickly, always the same decisive stride, looking for somewhere out of the way to sit before he'd even reached the bar. There weren't many folk inside so it suited him, the barmaid smiled, but there was something within her welcome that made him feel uneasy.

"You aren't from these parts?" Her eyes fixed on him a shade to long.

"I live Exeter way." Counting his money out.

"What you doing here then?"

Realising those about were listening, he played to her desire for more than chat. Letting his eyes run over her, while she smiled and simpered, getting flustered the more he played along. "Been visitin' family. Things are worse than Devon that's fer sure, so I'm off home, hoping I still have work."

The girl was clearly smitten and Jeremiah did not want the fuss.

"I can ask here if you would like? Mrs. Hardstaff was saying yesterday she needed two pair of hands. She is away a few days at the moment." Looking at him through a great deal of hope.

Jeremiah decided then upon a half truth, "I'll be straight with ye I had a falling out wi' a lass I were to wed," whispering it over the bar, "I'm hoping she'll have me back, if her damned family will let me near her."

The girl gave a rueful smile, "lucky lady, well if you have the need you can always call back this way." Grinning, then turning off to serve another customer.

The man nearest, with arms like barrels nudged him, seemingly amused by all of it. "You'd ha' no trouble like that wi' her, her family want shut, quick as can be." Laughing, then taking another swallow.

Flushing a shade of crimson, the young woman threw a curse across the bar. Those nearest no longer interested; so he was let alone apart from a few sly glances from his newly acquired friend.

Jeremiah smiled and turned away, to pick out a chair beside the fireplace. Where a ragged old man sat on the opposite side to look into an empty grate, nursing a jug of ale. Jeremiah watched a moment, while he rubbed his wrists, then shuffled about within his seat as though uncomfortable, to start the whole process off again.

No-one appeared to be interested in him or the old man either, so he was left to spend a pleasant evening, watching the man opposite who appeared to inhabit another world, rubbing at his wrists.

Time went on and he was so enjoying having a chair to sit in, he'd clean forgot he needed daylight to find a billet in the undergrowth.

The old man made his way towards the door, except for him the last to leave, his new friend following, seemingly impatient to lock up.

"Good night Tobias." And off the old man went, shuffling along, as if he didn't feel the need to move his legs more than was necessary. There was something about this that left a distinctly bitter taste. He turned his mind to where he was to sleep, then felt a tug upon his arm, a gentle voice left him with a smile.

"No one is here, cook left hours ago, so if you'd like to stay, it is no trouble. Truth is I do not like being here alone."

He thanked her profusely, making to sit in the chair he'd just vacated.

Ramming home the bolt upon the door, she spun around to laugh and beckon him forward. "I meant upstairs. There are beds, you don't need to pay."

The thought of a bed was way too much to leave alone, smiling he followed knowing others would have no trouble at all with this dilemma. Up the narrow, creaking stairs to her room, at the very top of the inn. When the candle was blown out, they both decided their best course was to keep to their clothes and share the bed; which was common practice among working folk if you couldn't afford a room of your own. The girl seemed completely taken with the idea that he loved another and made no more about it.

Morning came much too quickly, and sure enough his new acquaintance provided him with a hearty breakfast, while his pockets were filled to overflowing with bread and cheese. The poverty of the Midlands did not seem to stretch this far, in this way he set out for his journey with more heart than of late, but his mind was now on Ann. When he needed her the most, he could not help but feel in some small way he had betrayed her. Though he knew Ann well enough to know she was nothing if not a pragmatist, so settled himself to what was done out of necessity.

The young woman opened the door smiling gently. "If you go that way." Pointing to fields that appeared to run forever. They are done there for the moment, 'til they go in for harvesting, so there shouldn't be anyone about."

His smile faded.

"I knew who you was soon as you walked in, been reading all about it in't newspapers."

Jeremiah pushed back into the inn, the young woman lost her usual colour, nearly falling in an effort to pull away as quickly as she could.

"Don't be afraid miss, I owe you more than I can pay, and I would never wish to hurt a woman." How did no one else know? If it is common knowledge?" looking stunned.

Stammering at first the young woman recovered quickly. "I… gather papers up…when Mrs. Hardstaff's away, so I can read them at me leisure. Buggers pinch them if I don't,.. an I'm not that quick at reading as some." Calming a little. "It's not been in before, an' most don't buy one anyway, they come here an' read ours."

"May I see what they are sayin'?

Her smile fell to a sadness, "Just so's you know, I don't believe what they're writin', that you killed a man," her colour coming back to her.

Jeremiah said nothing, recognising an innocence that once was his, in another lifetime so very far away.

Hurrying off to fetch the newspapers she returned to stand in silence, while Jeremiah devoured the detail. To his dismay no other march went through that night, his had been the only force to trudged through the pouring rain. Now he realised the focus of the country would be upon his small army and the role that he had played. His hope the government would have so much to do searching up and down the country for all those intent upon reform had no foundation. They had been bought and sold it seemed, and now he had the answer, he was well capable of killing and if he could find that liar Oliver, he could show his new friend how to do it. In his case it seemed, that circumstance could make a killer and it could make one of us all, given time and opportunity. Truth was if he managed to kill William Oliver he would have felt much the better for it, his mind now in a torment only he could know.

Turning from the window. "Be best if you leave now." Her voice upon a higher pitch.

Along the road a cart wound its way steadily toward the inn. Jeremiah walked briskly to the door hoping to take his direction from her. Where does the road lead?"

She smiled. "To freedom and a better life, God's speed. Jeremiah."

More anxious than before, realising his true position but careful of his manners, knowing he should have asked. "Seeing that we are better acquainted. "What should I call you?"

The young woman laughed. "Rose, my name is Rose."

Lifting his hat, he tried but could not find a smile, "Thank you Rose. I am indebted to you. Maybe one day we will meet again." With that he left, to blend once again into the countryside, his new friend watching 'til there was no sign of him at all, whispering. "Maybe."

'Though Rose told him the directions he should take, he was not happy to used such tracks, so took a course through the fields, until no buildings could be seen.

A couple of days and he would be in Brighton, he had little option whether he should go or keep away, the only money he had was to get himself aboard any ship that might be persuaded to take him, not daring to call elsewhere now he knew the truth.

*

Standing by the end of the road his heart leapt, when a petite, perfectly groomed young woman came through the door. To sweep down the road, carrying a little wicker basket, turning into the shop upon the corner. It wasn't long before he stood watching her return, then walked steadily towards her, affecting a limp. The sweeping graceful movement of her gait turned to a faster pace, once through the door a delicate hand pulled him inside, to kiss him and throw her arms around him.

Jeremiah stepped back, conscious of how unkempt he was. "Well there's a welcome."

Looking him up and down a distressed smile greeting his arrival.

"I'm sorry to have come Mary, I suppose I don't smell too good either." His family were reasonably well off and he was conscious of it.

Dark eyes searched his own, "Jeremiah, tell me it is not true, that you have not done the things they say?" Grabbing his hand before he had the chance of a reply, taking him into the back room that led onto another. "Tell me what's happened?" Looking earnestly at him, "I am so glad to see you and know that you are safe."

He hesitated a moment, then the floodgate opened.

The horror of it not confined to what her brother had done; his sister sat pressing her hands into her dress. "Did you not think once to change your circumstance and come here instead of this?"

Shrugging he wasn't going to argue why he considered his actions just. To those who'd never felt such poverty, it seemed apparent they could not see why it should come to such a turn.

"We'd not money enough to eat some days, so a journey was impossible, parish relief does not stretch that far." He laughed. "I cannot remember the last time I had work." Shrugging. "And if I'm honest it never occurred to me other places would be different. Life here is very easy compared."

Mary smiled, but her distress was building. "If I understand you, many were thinking of a rising and may have done so in time, but this delegate from London appeared, and had the backing of those you trusted, and then began to instigate all of it?"

Jeremiah sighed. "It is the size of it."

His sister shook her head in disbelief, "While the authorities imprisoned the northern leaders two days before you marched, to leave you adrift, and all the time you were assured the country was to rise with you. This is the governments design and no mistake." Her face showed the horror she felt now and a dread that ran like ice around her veins.

"There must be a good number we trusted in their pay. They knew our plans, and waited on our move."

Mary nodded. "You must leave for other lands without delay, but you look so tired, this is not the work of weeks." Tenderly glancing his face with her hand. "What of Ann and the children?" She watched her brother swallow; feeling her heart would burst for all his pain.

"Ann is with her family, we agreed that she would leave the following day for Sutton. Truth is I know no peace since. If I can get to America, I can send for them given time." A cold anger overtook him. "I do not regret that night, only that we were deceived, they are murders, no more than killers for a coin, it is all they care for, they may dress in better clothes and call themselves our peers but they are little more than vermin. They do not care how many starve; indeed they set the wheels in motion to produce it, while those who work under that system cannot escape it. Surely if they were reasonable men they would pay enough for folk to feed their family, am I wrong Mary, to expect it so." He looked at his sister; then shook his head. "A weeks work for a few vegetables an' some rancid meat no one could eat, that is how we lived; the truth of it, how they had us by the throat. From the time there was light enough to work, five, six in the morning until dusk, at times a darker choice, between who ate and who did not. They did not need us then, they had the mills already built, they were just starving us into submission to fill their mills because they could. We were luckier than some; we had help from Ann's family when we were forced into the workhouse. Not long after the removal order came, we ended up in Nottingham we had furniture and bits to sell, Ann's mother pushed upon us. At the time I wondered what she was about, now I see she knew more than she said, it kept us going a good while. The odd occasion I found work mending someone else's frames helped, along wi' poaching. Not once Mary, no once did they deal fairly, week after week, there was no end to it. If you went into t' mills they'd built, the' had you just the same. No, my regret about that night is that I failed, but the reality was, we had no chance, from the moment we

set out. Yet I cannot help but think, if we had made it into
Nottingham; would it have changed things?" This anger drained
away, closing his eyes he put his head into his hands. Then looked
at his sister, resigned to what was done. "To leave this land and
those I love is the only hope I have of ever being with my family."

Wanting to ease his torment, Mary realised there was nothing
she could do to take this pain away, so she would do what she
could "stay by the fire, I'll bring a change of clothes." Cutting a
large piece of pie on the back dresser she pushed it towards him,
trying to hide the pain she felt, for he looked so ill and weary.
Hurrying into the adjoining room to hide behind the curtain, so he
would not see her tears.

It was much later in the evening when Mary's husband returned
home from work and she relayed everything to him.

Seeing how unhappy she was, he greeted Jeremiah with some
courtesy and warmth given the situation. Fortunately Jeremiah's
brother in-law had a steady inclination to do what he considered
right. After listening to how they'd lived he appeared aggrieved
that Jeremiah had never thought to visit them and get help.

When it was all explained he took this pain to himself, and felt
his anger hard to hold, on learning of such treatment. Seeing how
they were trapped in a cycle of despair they could not break.

Jeremiah was fortunate to spend a few days there, able to relax
in a manner he had not experienced in months, maybe years.
Having always been under the worry of where the work came
from, and whether it would be enough to feed them. The

difference now was he was being force fed to the point he had to protest he had eaten enough and was supplied with fresh clothing. Having deciding between them, they would get him to the vessels he needed now and from there he could escape to a better life,

On the day he was to leave a *Gig was brought into the yard with him hidden comfortably beneath the seat, it was a hundred and thirty miles to Bristol, so both knew the journey would take a few days. Once out in open country he would ride upon the bench beside his brother-in-law and share his hopes of how life might turn if he could get to other lands.

While his brother-in-law regaled him with tales of his wild youth and all the times he'd had, and how he happened to meet Mary.

Pressing a good few coins into Jeremiah's hand when they eventually parted company. Still unable to understand why he'd not brought his family to meet them long before now. Making their farewell with that sorrow hanging there.

Leaving Jeremiah to ponder while he walked down toward the quay whether he should have done that, but Ann was never keen to move from those she loved. Furthermore he never had the money for such a journey, even in the best of times. The children and Ann would have had to ride inside the coach and the journey down was more miles than he cared to think about at present. Though he'd tried to save enough for passage to America when times were brighter, it had never been enough. Neither could they have clung to the top of the coach holding onto baggage, but maybe he should have gone alone and things might have played out differently.

It was done now, however, there was little point in regret, though he would have felt he'd turned from those he stood with for all those years. Jeremiah was always filled with a higher purpose and it drove him still; there was no easy answer.

He stood watching the industrious work going on around the quay from a hidden corner. Slipping into the nearest inn, to stare out of the window at vessels that looked so majestic. The noise adding to the excitement, different orders being given. The quay was a hive of industry, everyone having an appointed role. After a while all of it became just another part of the scenery.

Feeling for the money inside his pocket, his mind wandered to those that walked beside him. Knowing many were now languishing in gaol, then thought of Ann, but could not carry into his mind his children, so stared as if transfixed at the work going on outside. At least Ann had family to shelter her, trying to settle his mind to getting on board and away from eyes that might claim reward.

Everything happened in a blur of negotiation, not ending the way he'd planned. Having got himself on board he was observed once the final preparations were under way and turned off with just enough money to try his luck again. For some reason he was not dismayed, his only course now was to seek out another vessel and see if it would take him, hoping he still had enough money to secure a different outcome.

*

It was well past midday when Jeremiah heard the bells and leapt into the undergrowth like a startled hare. After finding another vessel and bribing one of the crew, he was again observed and turned off. He hadn't the money they wanted, and they considered him a liability, thinking him not fit enough to work his passage, they were probably right. The years living on next to nothing and the weeks evading capture had taken their toll upon him, so a new life in America was not to be or at best on hold, though the money he had paid was not returned.

Consequently, he was now crouching in the undergrowth, the sound of distant bells coming ever closer. Watching with some pleasure the packhorses go past, their bells alerting all to their presence. It seemed a happy sight, but on examination he was reminded of his life, desperate and overworked for very little. The packs so weighed down he was left to wonder how much rest these animals got, watching them disappearing down the road and off into the distance.

Days blended into weeks, another and he hoped to be in Sutton. Wondering how Ann would receive him, it did not matter he had to see her, it was like opium to him, to tell her he would send for her once he was established and not to worry. He would find somewhere they'd be safe, lurching between despair and optimism.

Apart from those he knew in Sutton there was but one man he trusted now, knowing he might need more help with hiding out than Sutton would be in any position to provide. They'd known

114

each other five years and always managed to escape the
authorities. Remembering it was Henry that encouraged him to
attend the meetings in Nottingham years ago now, Henry did not
always gather what was said so well, so Jeremiah went along
when he appeared to want the company. Not too involved at first,
until he had to agree with everything they said, it being similar to
what his father told him years ago.

Watching the house not wanting to arrive if he was not there,
but with far more folk about than he wanted, he considered it
prudent to try his luck. He had wanted to go straight to Sutton but
was so tired he knew it wouldn't be best idea, for he would need
his wits about when he did, knowing the local constables would be
watching Bedlam Court.

Knocking upon the door he was greeted by amazement,
Sampson quickly set something to warm for him to eat, while
lifting pots of water to hang from the hooks above the fire, to fill
the tub before it, his guest stood shaking inside his sodden clothes.

It had rained continuously all day and much of the night before,
reminding Jeremiah of the march. The smell of warming soup
was now almost too much to bear. Henry seeing he was shaking
handed him the soup and bread, to watch while he devoured it.
When the tub was half filled, Jeremiah ripped off his clothes to
wash them, while Henry stood beside the blaze to keep it going.

"What day is it Henry?"

"It is Saturday the nineteenth of July my friend." Leaning
across to pass him the washboard, highly amused by the whole

scene.

Jeremiah shook his head. "I will never be able to re-pay you, you have my thanks; unfortunately I have no more to give. I had to sell all to any peddler that passed in exchange for food. It's six weeks since that night, it feels like years." rubbing his clothes up and down against the board.

Henry's smile disappeared, unnoticed by his guest, who looked in the direction of the knitting frame. "I've had good fortune recently," the smile broadened again. A relative I hardly knew, left enough money to make life easy, so the machine is silent, there's still little work to be had."

Jeremiah stepped from the tub, to dry himself. "I am glad for you Henry, truly. It heartens me that someone is in receipt of good fortune." The words were truly meant.

Henry moved the conversation onto how his guest had managed to evade the authorities for quite so long. Throwing Jeremiah's dripping clothes over a towel and couple of iron bars that hung from the ceiling above the fire for the purpose. "You should be sailing to America by now?" Pulling the tub underneath them.

His guest shrugged, still torn between what should have been and what he desired the most. Having someone to talk to was a huge relief, but he was never inclined to talk of others, even with someone as close as Henry Sampson.

The next morning he awoke to feel a gut churning excitement at the prospect of seeing Ann and the children, only to have to wait 'til evening, time dragging on and when the light began to turn he set off.

On reaching the little town he hid, half crouching in a darkened corner behind the butchers yard on Beggar Street, to study those whose job it was to search out a fugitive that might visit Bedlam Court. Watching men he knew go past but dare not speak too. With more constables about than even he expected, he moved a few yards further on, to stand within the shadows by the orchard wall, watching where they went. The inns were starting to turn out, so he drifted in behind a group who never realised he was there. Then turned quickly into the small yard behind the Durham Ox, an inn he always used in other days, when a constable strolled by he'd not expected. To watch and wait, two more walked briskly past, keeping tight to the cottage walls to cross Criers yard, and then turn for Bedlam Court. A slight tap and the light went out, the door opened and George Bridget hauled him inside before he could even speak.

After trying to compose himself, George whispered, "Hey lad tha' should be miles away on't boat somewhere. But I am rate glad to si' thee." Thee like a son t' us tha' knows." shaking his head looking anguished, fearing this was not his safest move.

Acknowledging what was said Jeremiah smiled. "I'm glad to see yu' George. How's Ann and children?"

The collier's eyes caught all the hurt etched in that moment on his face, and turned without answering, to go up the narrow stairs. 'I'll get her lad." Realising that these were stolen moments and very likely the last time they would ever meet.

Jeremiah stood, to listen to every tiny sound, hearing her gentle tread upon the stairs, his heart soaring above all that went before.

The long nightshirt and halo of falling tresses hung about her, her feet on tiptoe after racing down the stairs so quickly she felt that she was flying, to stop at the sight of him. They stood gazing one upon the other, no smile, no show of emotion; the mirror image of when he came to tell her, he would lead that fateful march. In a rush they were in each other's arms, Ann drawing back looking distressed at how thin he looked.

Only then did Jeremiah smile, and place his hand upon the tiny bump that told him of a growing babe.

Stretching to kiss him, her hands either side of his face, reading his thoughts. "If I told you I'd discomfort with our babe, that truth was at that time, it was just a guess that I was caught, what then? But I did not; do not hold yourself at such high judgment. You did what you thought right, like you have always done. If those you held in regard behaved as well, you would not be standing here feeling such pain," her smile soothing the hurt she saw.

Seeing how tired he was Ann pulled him to the chair, stoking the fire into life. Then went to fetch something from the pantry, insisting that she sat beside him on the floor, knowing these hours may be all she would have to hold onto in the future. When he'd eaten they crept like teenagers half giggling, up the narrow stairs. To walk into the bedroom and go over to the children, both fast asleep, 'til Ann didn't think he'd ever move, to find his eyes full of tears, so pulled him back to sit upon the bed. "They will always know how much you love them and what you risked to make a better life, I promise. And we will come to you when it is safe." Her hands stole upwards, to wipe away the pain.

He realised then more must be said. "I will find somewhere I swear."

Laying her head upon his shoulder the pragmatist held sway. "There will never be a day I do not think of you, or remind the children of the times you played with them rolling round upon the floor." Laughing at the thought of it. "Do not forget us Jeremiah."

Closing his eyes just for a moment he sighed "When the ships would not take me, I had to be certain you were safe, and see it for myself. If they find me Ann, do not pine for what has gone, it is not what I would want, there will be no pardon."

"Why do you say such?" Pulling away, distressed, "why would you say that? If they find you, they may send you to other lands, I could come to you in time?"

"Ann please, listen to me and do not forget it. We have always told each other the truth haven't we, and been honest? It is and should be, no different now." Pulling her back to hold her, trying to calm this distress he saw. "If things do not go well, distance yourself from what's been done. They will watch you Ann and I know you, better than you know yourself, look to yourself then and the children, do not let their world or yours be one of sorrow." Looking at them nestled so warmly in their bed.

Silent tears slipped from those hazel eyes he'd watched so often before they met, he now looked into earnestly. "They have not set up such a trap to let us go, remember only the times we sat laughing by the dam. The nights we danced upon the Green, the old man playing on the fiddle while we sang. Plying the Romani's with drink to try to get the better of their tricks, sitting around the fire 'til late into the night, they are the times we must remember now, until we meet again. The times Reuben baited Bill, after losing his wages on their tricks, 'til Bill could stand it no more." Laughing pulling her close, "we are the richer for them and must hold them the dearer now."

Ann smiled at the thought of it, but didn't say what she was thinking, for those times seemed very distant. Shaking herself back into the present, "If anyone can do this it is you. I know it." Her hands shaking, for he was right, she had begun to deny everything, to help manage her fear, making out things were not quite so bad, so she could smile again.

Wiping away her tears, he held her tight the night overtaking them.

Next morning Ann woke to find her husband sound asleep, so crept out of the bed to stand a moment gazing at him, still handsome through all he had endured, leaving the bedroom quietly to let him rest.

When the children found their father lying there beside them, there was much joy, 'though they knew nothing of the risks he'd taken that he might see them. After a great deal of playing and rolling about upon the bed, Jeremiah came down the stairs carrying Timothy, little Lizzie quite recovered from the coughing, jumping before him like she always did when she was happy.

Finding his hosts sat around the table deep in conversation, Ann's siblings having been turned out early, so did not know they had a guest. He looked but said nothing; it was an image he would keep within his mind, smiling a moment at them.

"We were talkin' ah what is best. The south is risky, if you went into Wales, the' have no love for t' judiciary there; there'd be less interest I'd a thought. We've news the' watching Liverpool." George studied him.

"I cannot stay here, I will head back to Henry's," he shrugged.

At this revelation Ann could not hold her surprise. "Henry Sampson, you stayed with him?"

"Just the other night. He said he could shelter me a few days while I see if there is any help to be had. And offered a good amount to help me, he's had good fortune recently." Putting Timothy to the floor, the children ran into the other room to play.

"Which gives us time to raise enough for t' passage." George interrupted. "It 'ud be unwise to come back here, it's like a nest a wasps some days looking for thee. An' folk talk, even if the' mean no harm." Anyroad, we need a place no one bar us know, so I can meet thee. I'm certain we can raise a bit knowin' how folk are feelin' on't subject."

Jeremiah nodded and smiled. "Tell them they have my thanks and always will. We need somewhere you go already so we don't attract attention."

Knowing where he meant George's face lit up. "Aye *Ard'ick, I go most weeks since James Riggott died, his son Joseph runs inn now wi' his mother, 'tis perfect of an evening, wi' Duke in residence at Hall, they'll not expect ya' there. "You remember when we walked that time, when me lad o celebrated his coming of age up at Hall. The' went past in that big fancy coach by Rowthorne? An' we walked down hill t' ponds."

He smiled at the recollection. "It means going out the way a bit, but I would sooner keep to routes I know if I can. An' you know I like the walkin." Jeremiah grinned.

"I sit opposite Miller's pond most times I go, then walk over to Cockshutt woods, near Gin close, so it'll be no different to any other week, Wednesday evening after they've done in't quarry. Make sure tha' keeps away from inn, there's hangers on, an' t' forelock tugging brigade there. The' hold vestry meetings in't back an' overseer comes to sort accounts; we don't want 'um seeing you. Mind by time the' come out, the' rat arsed, so even if the' see you the' ne'er goin' t' remember. Near Gin Close, you'll not be seen there in't evening, there's a couple a huge trees near, I'll wait there for thee. It's where I sit most times."

Looking far more worried than before Ann could not hold back. "Stay here, Sampson always wants to know too much."

Shaking his head in disbelief but not wanting an argument, Jeremiah sighed. "I know you've never liked him, but I have known Henry for years now. Truth is they may come at any moment and search this house. I should not have come? It is good of Henry to offer. He says there's been a few taken up already, committee men, Mr. Holmes unfortunately and William Stevens is nowhere to be found, but Henry thinks the trail is cold now."

George agreed. "It is not safe for Jerry to stay here, not for him or thee an' t' children, us either. The' have searched this house from top to toe when you come here, dost tha' not remember? Whose t' say the' not come back? Though I would like it different you know that."

Biting back her frustration Ann tried to busy herself, hardly able to breathe for the disquiet she felt; then could not hold her fear any longer. "Explain to me then, why so many have been taken up and after folk were twisted in an' oaths said, so them that's doin' it have no problem with their lyin'." Somebodies informing and the person that's doing it's been on the inside all along and still is, or how did they know where to find us? They came to ours in Nottingham day after you'd marched, then straight to Alexander's, how did they know that, know exactly where to go?"

The room fell to a strained silence, all taking an unspoken decision to discontinue the discussion.

Jeremiah sent Ann a questioning stare, letting out a sigh to settle beside the fire. While George tapped his fingers on the table, giving his daughter a steely glare she studiously ignored, her heart beating out a rhythm of its own.

Ann's worries were not calmed any, but wanting to make the peace she went to sit upon the floor to lean against her husbands legs. While he looked into the fire, turning back to smile at her. "Are you recovered?"

"I know you think I'm wrong and I hope it is so, but I do not for one minute think it's for the best." Looking away again so he could not see her fear.

"I cannot stay here Ann, and if you sit upon the floor a moment longer I will leave. If they came, they could take you all, yet I could not keep away. I will send for you as soon as it is safe."

Ann pulled the little stool across to sit close up beside him, leaning her head against his shoulder.

"And I realise of course I cannot trust a word you say." His fingers playing lightly in her hair

Bursting out laughing, having stayed longer in Nottingham than she'd promised. "You cannot say that, Lizzie's chest was playing up, I did not know what to do. Beside my mind was all over the place, I could not think."

Still unnerved, but not wanting to add to his worries "Anyhow who should you turn to? And you may reprimand me all you like, all those men lying in gaol, someone from that committee knows more than they are saying. They should have called things off when they realised things were turning, but they left you, all of you, to carry the weight of it."

"Ann please, I dare say someone, somewhere is telling tales, but most are just as I and wanted a better life for folk. I will stay a few nights at Henry's no more, then make for Hardwick by the paths your father uses. No one will think it is any other than what he does every week." Smiling at her. "And I'll not tell Henry where I'm heading, will that make you happy?"

Resigning herself to it, "I will be happy when you're safe. I wish to God you'd stayed upon that boat."

"You want rid of me Ann?" Grinning at her.

Her worries were not so easily dismissed; picking herself up she could not answer, so went into the other room to see what the children were doing. With Jeremiah there she dare not let them in the yard for fear they said something they shouldn't.

There was a loud knocking at the door, Ann's mother hurried past to glance out of window, without saying a word opened the door, to a sharp intake of breath from those inside.

Bill stood smiling at them, then walked through to talk to George, making a silly face at the children, reaching the back room he stood a moment with his mouth open. Then raced across to grab Jeremiah by the shoulders. "We'd heard, northern leaders were taken up near Dewsbury on't seventh.' Bloody hell man, you've lost some meat, you're like a hanged hare an no mistake." Instantly embarrassed by what had just tumbled from his mouth.

Jeremiah grinned. "I'm very glad to see you Bill."

Ann walked into the room behind him, looking heavenward shaking her head as if he were the stupidest child in the classroom.

All three laughing at each other, then sitting at the table, in earnest discussion, the children running in and out to check their father was still there.

Jeremiah's mind was set, he would head for Birmingham, then

into Wales. Anywhere immediately west led him straight through Derbyshire and it was a route he had no desire to take.

Bill stood, then shook Jeremiah firmly by the hand, and took his leave of them. "God's speed my friend. I'll tell no one you're here, not even Sal. An' you'll have t' money tha' needs, I'll make sure on it. Send us a letter an' tell us what it's like over there eh." Pressing a few coins into his palm. "It were to get some at for Sal, but she'd want you to have it. When you're ready money will be here; dun't worry, I know who I can trust." Then walked out.

It was agreed Jeremiah would wait for George near Gin Close just up from Miller's pond, well beyond the Hardwick Inn where the coaches stopped, in a few days time. George met his kin at the inn and went each week to sit just down from Gin Close to enjoy the peace and quiet.

With the new coaching routes opening up, Hardwick wasn't quite as busy as before; the inns offering food and lodging were taking all the trade. Coaches went around eight miles an hour; mail coaches were faster not having to stop at any tolls. They were even more expensive, not only did you have to pay to travel, you paid the guard a shilling every thirty miles besides.

George said naught, but was hoping to get enough money together to secure Jeremiah at least one journey by coach. After looking at him, he didn't think he'd have the strength to travel all that way on foot, but knowing Jeremiah it was possibly the last thing he would want.

The next day seemed to pass so quickly there was nothing

anyone could say to make this exit any easier; Ann was starting to shake so much she could not stop. Knowing by the way her husband acted that time was now upon them. Turning, she picked up Timothy. "Your father must leave and may not be back for quite a while, so we must kiss him and wish him God's speed till we meet again." Setting him upon the floor, the children raced toward their father, who pulled them up one in each arm, kissing them while they clung with all their might about his neck.

Ann turned from the scene her sense of dread growing, but knew she must not cry. In a moment's remembrance, she picked up the water pail. "Well, if any were man enough, they could carry this for me." Smiling, though her eyes felt all but dead.

Setting the children down Jeremiah walked across to take the pail and place it down beside her, his hands either side of her face, gently stroking back her hair. "I never told you did I, that I'd watched you ever since I came here. It seems so long ago, but I would not trade one moment of our time together, for any time without you." He smiled. "Look after the children Ann and God willing I will do the best I can, so one day we can be together, all of us." Placing his hand upon her stomach. "And I am truly sorry, I let you down."

Ann gazed into those warm brown eyes "You never let me down, you're more a man than any one a them. It is they who let you down, along with those in gaol, leading all into a trap. It is not coincidence those of that committee are not where you stand now. They sensed the truth two days before you marched and let you risk all and those from Derbyshire."

"You know that is not true Ann, many are already taken up."

Untying a silken black scarf from about her neck she placed it lovingly round his. Thinking of the times he stood to let her do this. Though she knew he often felt a little smothered by the gesture, especially if Joe or Rueben were about, but had always smiled when it was done.

Today how much he needed it.

Ann shrugged then smiled again, for the scarf looked so very fitting upon him. "It is how I feel and nothing you say will change it."

Raising his eyebrows he smiled, then shook his head and laughed; he would never change her or her stoic support either; seeing the time was hard on her, he went quickly into the other room to make his goodbyes.

Ann's mother sat beside the fire holding all her tears.

"I will send for them, don't worry. Look after them for me." Smiling at both of them.

George marched briskly across to shake Jeremiah's shoulders in a manly fashion. "I'll see you lad at agreed spot, I have a plan to throw 'um if I'm followed. If you're longer I'll wait, an' come next day, at same time an' next."

Jeremiah nodded then grinned. "I do not plan on being late." Slipping into the back room he picked up the children one at a time, to kiss them. "Be good for your mother, look after her, stroking Lizzie's long brown hair, to share a smile and kiss her once again, then ruffling his fingers through Timothy's mop of curls, making the faces that always made him laugh. For some reason Timothy did not laugh, instead he looked earnestly at his father. Ann seeing this took him into her arms and let him kiss his father on the lips, gathering Lizzie to her.

Another hug for Ann; kissing her gently on the side of her face, finding that he could hardly speak.

"God's speed my love." Trying to look confident, smiling the best she could.

With her words ringing in his ears he crept out of the door and away.

*Jennel : Narrow alleyway, usually between terraced houses.

*'Ard'ick: Hardwick

Chapter Seven

MINTED IN BLOOD

Henry Enfield, the town clerk hurried from behind his desk to shake the hand of his informant vigorously, a huge smile emblazoned across his face.

Having been in the employ of the town clerk for the best part of five years, this would be the biggest payday his informant would ever have.

A great deal of self-congratulatory applause ran around Enfield's office, while the informant stood to one side largely ignored by all within the now enlivened room. Those inside decided the forthcoming result was well worthy of a toast, saving their formal celebrations for when this trap was sprung.

Tipping his hat towards them the informant closed the heavy door very quietly behind him. Slipping away unnoticed, not having been invited to partake, taking a familiar route, down a dirty alleyway to the main thoroughfare. Indeed those inside the room never even noticed his departure. He was left to consider the coin he would receive if this plan went well, knowing how to barter on such matters for he'd had years of practice.

After the Nottingham Captain's arrival in Bulwell on the twentieth of July, the price upon him rose, exceeding more than many earned inside a year.

Turning from the filthy alleyway, the informant stood a moment to make sure no-one from the North Midland Committee or his

Luddite days just happened to be passing.

Walking quickly through the streets until he reached the inn, making sure his entrance there was noted. Once settled in his usual seat he began to hum one of the old Luddite songs, 'til he was told to hush his mouth by those he sat beside, almost like a child, clamouring for their attention. The chair empty on his left; where a friend sat in brighter times than this. Every now and then a shiver travelled his spine sitting amongst those who would not have taken it so well if they had known where he had been. A moment every now and then found its way to his regret, for Henry liked the victim well enough. Remembering how he'd saved him from the soldiers the night they met, coming from his hiding place to pull him down a hidden *jennel. That, however, was before Henry turned to other ways of earning, but times were hard and he had numerous children al of whom needed feeding, yet somehow this felt different. Not for the first time, however, his pockets would overflow with coin minted in blood, but if those he sat with knew, it would surely be the last.

Strange though it was, no one from the committee ever suspected Henry Sampson, not then at least.

*

Two and half hours after leaving Sutton on the twenty second of July, Jeremiah stood to one side in a darkened alleyway watching the streets of Bulwell. There were few people about so he considered it best to wait until the inns were closing and follow on. Slipping in behind a group of lads coming around the corner, he was soon through the door at Henry's. Standing to look about him when no one appeared to be home, certain Henry said he'd be there, but if he wasn't he had said to let himself in. Going over to the fire that looked like he hadn't been there for a while. Placing a few bits of wood upon it to keep it going, gently teasing a little air underneath with the poker. Not having lit any candles, he could still see the room was well furnished; unlike their lodgings back in Nottingham. Walking over he took a look at the knitting frame that stood idle in the corner. Most spending every hour they had upon their frames if they were fortunate enough to have the work.

There was a loud knocking at the door; he had no weapons, having sold everything he'd carried. The rapping became louder more persistent, going through the back he could hear footsteps someone was coming up the yard. A cold dread descended when he walked calmly to the door.

"We've been told there's snares here, out the way." One man pushed through, going straight to the back door, another stayed as if on guard. The door to the back yard was then forced open, they gave a peremptory search, turning to look him up and down, the moment seemed to last an age. Then like he wasn't hearing them. "Jeremiah Brandreth you are under arrest."

Nothing felt real from that moment on, he was staring into the space before him while they bound his hands and walked him out of the house.

It wasn't long before he was stood between three men; certain one was the magistrate that rode after them that night. Saying nothing, in contrast to the excitement they seemed to feel. Trying not to think, then he was led quickly into a darkened room with no window, his bindings undone and a jug of water and some bread left on a low concrete area to the side. Having been informed he would be taken to Derby gaol and await trial there. Wondering if the men there would accept him or would they consider all of it his fault?

After a while he realised someone else was near and went over to the grill upon the door to look into the face of a man in the cell opposite, his hair bedraggled and unkempt. The moment he saw Jeremiah, he started on his tale.

"I did not kill her the' sayin that I killed her, but she were dead. They will hang me, an' God is my witness, I ne'er killed her. But none on 'um believe me, I took her shoes an' that umbrella. I ne'er took her life, an Bessie Shepard didn't need 'um, that's what the' called her, so I could sell 'um, t' get somethin' t' eat." This carried on well into the night.

Jeremiah knew Bessie, for they lived in the same town, till he was forced to leave it. Giving the only comfort that he could, never telling the tormented soul he knew her. "Well if it helps thee, I believe you." A lump began to grow inside his throat, he felt himself slithering down the door to sit the rest of the night his back toward it. Not feeling the need for further conversation he had troubles enough of his own, thinking of a young girl very like his daughter but all grown up, who deserved much more from life than that.

He sat going over all that he had done, thinking of his gaoled army knowing William Turner had been taken quickly; it crossed his mind William and those in gaol might be fortunate now. Not having 'drawn the badger,' might allow them their freedom instead of harsher penalty. In some strange way he felt reconciled to what was happening, as if he knew it would come to this all along. Then thought how Ann would take the news, knowing it would not be well, he buried his head in his hands, unable to think of anything except her and his little babes.

The next morning, he was transferred early to Derby gaol, maybe they feared a plot to free him. Smiling to himself, they need not have bothered, no one called off the march, so it was unlikely anyone cared enough to free him.

He was held for a few minutes in a bleak room, to meet the gaoler and some he had no intention of bothering to know. Then bundled through to the exercise area, to look around him, yet couldn't recognise one person.

There were so many in there, the gaoler insisted they went into the yard, so they were stood in small groups talking, it was then he recognised a few and nodded. Like that evening six weeks ago, George Weightman strode toward him smiling, "Captain."

Holding out his hand while Jeremiah juggled his emotions, thinking where the night had led them. Though he thought of them often, when plainly before you it was so very different. One by one they came to shake his hand and ask why on earth he was not on his way to America. The truth was inexplicable, why hadn't he tried harder to remain aboard, would it have made a difference, had he risked all to see his family again after walking all that way, the odd ride in the back of some wagon having helped?

Strangely the man he felt most affinity with was not the first to greet him, William Turner stood at the back of the group looking searchingly at him. After a time he like all the rest asked how he'd evaded capture quite so long. When he told them he'd managed to get aboard two vessels in the hope of getting to America to be turned off both, their surprise and dismay knew no bounds.

George Weightman though, went around telling everyone that would listen their Captain would not let them carry the penalty alone.

Jeremiah knew he had never courted this detainment, even if he gained release like those in Yorkshire, which he doubted, his only hope of any kind of life was one well away from England. There was of course the conundrum of whether he shot Robert Walters, who might have been coming out to join them. Whether he was or wasn't really didn't matter, it had the same unfortunate ending, had some other gun discharged within the house, they were unlikely to say? He did, however, consider if he'd spilt blood his own were forfeit, but to all other questions, he did not have an answer? His regret lay within the fact that the rising was not what he'd been told. No Northern clouds of marching men appeared on the horizon, having been halted days before; no seventy thousand in London were waiting there to rise, only his small army marching towards ruin. He could not answer whether he would have marched if he had known the truth, it was too hard to contemplate; he could only bring himself to consider what was done. Whatever else he decided should be between his own convictions and the Lord. Being a committed Baptist, he held a strong belief in the Lord's justice and no one else could decide upon it.

*

It was not until the evening of the twenty-third, that Bill knocked upon the door at Bedlam Court. George was getting ready for a bath, wiping himself down with an old towel in the backyard taking most of the dust away. While Elizabeth stooped to pick up his clothes giving them a good shake, then throwing them into another tub to soak, coming close he bent to kiss her.

Pushing him away laughing, "ger' off ya', daft ha'peth," rubbing at the dirt upon her cheek. The girls giggling, while John turned off in disgust, George strode into the house to answer the knocking at the door. Hannah and her brother having just returned with yet another pail of water, while Martha and Liz rubbed the clothes against the washboard. Lifting and repeating, helped by two pairs of tiny hands and much laughter, Timothy already soaking wet, determined he would drench his sister no matter what was said against it.

Half clothed, his outer garments lying stiff with dust in the backyard or already in the tub, George gained the door.

Ann glanced across, turned to fill the bathtub.

A huge pot of stew bubbled away, hanging from a sturdy iron bar within the chimney, from which numerous pot-hooks were suspended, to take the different pots and pans. Walking to the washbowl, after another pan of water was left to warm over the fire, looking at her father to see his hand go to wall, to leave a blackened imprint there.

Realising there was something very wrong; she walked towards him, like her legs belonged elsewhere.

George turned to place his arm about her, while Bill stood upon the doorstep like a crumpled letter, bent under the weight of a message he had no desire to tell. "I'm sorry Ann, I came soon as I heard, the' went looking for snares at Sampson's an' recognised him."

Ann pulled away, to spit out her thoughts out like they were bullets from a gun. "Oh! I bet. They had no need for snares, they had their game already trapped." Looking accusingly at both of them. "I told you he's is a Judas, I told you all, an' no one, not one of you would listen." Running off into the street.

George tried his best to stop her. "Ann, think a the baby," the words drifting upon a silence that began to wrap itself around the town.

Unable see where she was going, wanting to outrun the day, wind back the clock and shield all she loved from harm.

Sal was sat upon the Green, feeling distress, her life untouched by the devastation those around her suffered. To see Ann there so got up hurriedly to grab a hold of her before she fell. Both half-tumbling on the grass beside the little river, Sally fumbling for a handkerchief, tucked inside her sleeve to dry Ann's the tears, and wrap her arms around her, while Ann still poured forth her accusations.

Strange enough Sal could see the truth in every word. "Why is it men cannot see what is so obvious to us?" Feeling Ann's despair Sal held her tight, then helped to her feet. "There's but one place can help us." Walking across the empty Green, by the Manor House, to the Church that held so many happy memories, hoping it could be a source of comfort to her.

Ann remembered happier times when she had taken her father's arm upon her wedding day. How fortunate she felt that Jeremiah loved her and how handsome he had looked just waiting there. The image took a hold inside Ann's mind, Jeremiah turning to smile as she arrived, the tender look within his eyes that so enchanted her, played over and over now. How proud she felt and something stirred that same pride, to gain a strength beyond any she'd expected and in that way she began to steel herself for a future that would very likely be without him.

Praying with every fibre of her being it would be gaol or he would be transported nothing worse. Knowing if that should happen she'd never see him again, but it was better than the rope. Considering Jeremiah would be right; they would not be as fortunate as those in Yorkshire and freed to go back to their family. Kneeling to make a promise, she would tell her children the truth, for she felt certain others would. Recalling her embarrassment having to put her mark with a cross when they were wed, not knowing how to write. How elated she felt when she saw her name and his together, the curate, Thomas Hurt writing it for her.

In the years that followed Jeremiah tried to teach her all her letters, though Ann was none too interested. Allowing it because he would sit so close beside her, she could almost feel his heart beat, his arm about her, his hand over her own. While Sal would look at the delight upon her face and burst out laughing, knowing exactly what Ann was up too. In that way she learnt a little; but Ann had an extraordinary capacity to remember lines of verse and she would trick Jeremiah into thinking she had read some long dialogue on occasion. Laughing fit to burst when he discovered that was not the case.

Never once, thinking it was not worth his time, always too serious for his own good. Most of her background did not know how to read or write, it had never worried her before thinking that she'd never need it, now she realised it was all she had, and would have written letter after letter until her hands bled if she could. Wondering what she could say to God he did not know that might bring her generous loving husband back to her.

Sally knelt not quite sure what she should say, hoping God might extend his mercy to Jeremiah and give Ann the comfort she so needed now.

They'd walked into St. Mary's holding each other's hand, the way they had when they were little, hoping to find God listening, 'til they could ask no more.

Nothing, though, could stop the painful yearning Ann felt for the man she held within her arms just hours ago.

The strength that came from walking into the Church she loved would be a source of comfort to her she could call on in the future.

Walking down the aisle, she lifted Sally's hand to kiss it, and thank her. "I don't know how I'd be without you Sal, both laughing at each other through their tears.

Sal smiled at her. "Most were let off up north, said it was a riot nothing more, surely we can hope for the same." But at the back of Sal's mind the whispers they were hearing, whether an accident or not, lay like cloud that would not go away.

Ann remembered Jeremiah's counsel, walking by the site of the Luddite attack, down the incline to the little river, and over the stepping-stones.

Holding her stomach, grinning at Sal a small happiness intruded on their pain. Along Beggar Street, past the orchard and the strangely silent inn's, up to Bedlam Court, the town wrapped in her sorrow as if it was their own.

Before opening the door, Sal gave a smile, Bill came across to give Ann an uncomfortable manly hug.

"You all right? I'm sorry, it were not the news I wanted to give thee." Looking despondent and sheepish all at the same time, as if he were solely to blame for all of it.

She smiled and hugged him, whispering something no one else could hear, Bill usually did not know the right thing to say, but it was always from the heart, and surprisingly what was needed now which made Ann grin all the more, knowing her husband loved him like a brother.

Jeremiah's Uncle stood very upright beside her father, and came across, he was a stout handsome man, very dark like Jeremiah. "I am sorry lass, I were keeping away, not knowing how you'd be feelin', but I couldn't in't end. I hope they are treated similar t' other's an' returned to their families."

Ann smiled, "I am and always will be proud of Jeremiah; though I will mind my counsel for the sake of our babes."

Looking at her through a mix of pride and worry. He sighed. "Lass, do not fight a battle tha' cannot win. Though, I am proud of him and love him like my own, I know he'd want to take that burden from you, not leave you shackled to it. You have family, do not forget you have us. I'll leave you be, but if you've need of us, do not forget it." He sighed. "We must pray he is returned to us." Picking his cap up from the sideboard he walked out, closing the door behind him.

Sal said her farewells, pulling Bill along to walk dejectedly home holding his hand without a word.

Bill and Sally married soon after they met and were living with Sal's parents, the cottage being big enough to house them all. Bill was now better off than he had ever been, which left him to consider how fate had played their lives. Not having gone a Ludding except for the attack at Smedley's End, now he was grateful for it. Never feeling the need, but then his former master paid him well, so he'd been luckier than most.

Having the smallholding and Sal's father ailing, he had all the work he needed, but not enough to take on help and even in abject poverty Jeremiah seemed so very self reliant, Bill never dared to ask. Therefore, he would never now the answer to a question that would vex him all his life.

*

Ann sat upon the floor beside her mother holding her hand, telling her where she'd been and how she could not think what else to do. "What do I tell the children, that their father is in gaol, if I say nothing, someone will, you can be sure. They will not understand it anyway?"

"Wait a while, we will protect them for the moment, no one knows what will happen." Elizabeth gave her daughter a gentle smile and rubbed her hand. "They are in the yard at present, John is showing them everythin' he shouldn't splashing everyone last time I looked. I've told him not to splash our Lizzie. They are happy, indeed spoilt a little I do not doubt."

"Do you mind if I go upstairs and try to think what I should say to them?"

Elizabeth looked far older than her years. "Aye lass, you take your time. There's no rush."

After an hour going over everything, ending up at the beginning, Ann realised, however, long she stayed up there nothing was going to change. The children were still playing, she sat upon the bed trying to gather enough wit to be near them.

142

Listening when her mother brought them from the yard, telling them not to disturb her for she was tired. It was nothing to worry about, just something that happened when babies grew.

Ann heard a thousand questions being fired, her sisters much the same, full of an excitement she could not share at present, a treasure she would love in spite of everything when that moment came.

Lizzie was now four and Timothy nearly two; their interest in the baby was akin to their delight at Christmas. Both taken with an urgent desire to be with their mother, making everybody laugh.

Timothy tried his best to scurry past them.

"Come here little man," his grandmother lifting him wriggling from the floor, their childish antics drying everyone's tears.

George smiled, taking Timothy from his wife to place him firmly on his knee. "Now then young 'un. Timothy stopped his wriggling to stare at his grandfather a moment as if he knew he'd overstepped the boundary. "Dada."

George gazed at him. "Ay' you are his son and that's for sure," sighing quietly, he placed the little boy to the floor, his determination noted. "She needs 'um more than we do, I reckon."

Lizzie jumping with excitement as if the baby were already there, somewhat aggrieved Timothy might get upstairs before her.

It had all gone strangely quiet; Ann was about to pick herself up and go downstairs, having heard only bits of their conversation.

A small noise at the bedroom door caught her attention, four tiny chubby fingers and a mass of black brown curls stuck out beside it. In seconds two button black bright eyes were peeping at her around the door. The minute he saw his mother's smile upon him, he ran full pelt into her arms. In one joyous moment Ann knew whatever came, she would have her husband with her in her children and her heart was shown a light she could hold and cherish. In seconds a small image of herself entered the room arms folded, like a Sunday School teacher with a disruptive class, eyes on Timothy all pomp and ceremony, making her mother laugh out loud. Pulling them both onto the bed beside her, tickling them till they were laughing as if her husband were still there. Ann's course was clear she must take the role her husband played, the role at times she had resented. Seeing now so very clearly though he could not provide the comforts others had, or enough food to eat, he had so often lifted their hearts with laughter and a love beyond price.

Chapter Eight

GOODNIGHT TOBIAS

Unbeknown to the men in gaol, discussions were on going behind the scenes on the part of the judiciary, in the form of who was to be tried for what. Some considered a few might be tried on the highest charge in the land, High Treason, but word came back as many would be tried upon the charge they might be able to convict. Habeas Corpus, having been suspended months ago, they could be held however long the government wanted on a diet of bread and water.

It was then decided they would not proceed until the harvest was gathered; which ironically was to be a good one, unlike the previous year. They could therefore fill the jury with rich farmers and landed gentry who would not be put out any by losing their crops.

Everyday more men were brought into the gaol, so many they could not lie to sleep, forcing them into sleeping upright shoulder to shoulder. Within days of the Nottingham Captain being delivered to the prison, he was taken from the yard.

The men waited not knowing what was happening, they soon had the answer, Jeremiah was returned with heavy irons upon his feet and wrists, akin to a marionette without the strings, making life even more difficult and any comfort rare, although he'd not been tried yet.

With so many prisoners, the gaoler became concerned that they would try to force their way out, with only his wife and four men to deal with anything that might ensue.

The men need not have worried their Captain had been singled out for special treatment, for George Weigthman, William Turner and Isaac Ludlam were all led off to receive the very same treatment.

There was, however, some good news, they were to be given better fare, having existed on bread and water thus far. Their solicitor had asked if they might be allowed proper meals, the reply came back that they could have a meal according to their station. Jeremiah having been there around two and a half weeks, concerns were growing many would not make it to trial; one man already so ill he was released from prison within days.

Then a day of great dismay, the four prisoners that fired Colonel Wingfield Halton's hayricks were to hang. Some thought the sentence would be quashed, but that never happened. Two, at least in Jeremiah's view were but boys, George Booth twenty-one, Thomas Jackson twenty, John King twenty-four, and John Brown thirty-eight. Both he and William Turner observed one to the other, it was a mistake not to have "Drawn the Badger" when they had the chance.

They stood in the exercise yard watching all that was to happen, when a heavy shower preceded the event, two of the younger lads retreated under an umbrella, at which the crowd's laughter cut all who heard. When the drop was upon them Jeremiah found himself chanting silent prayers for those about to suffer. The horror of this scene and what could be in store for them presented itself with brutal clarity. Then silence, followed by derision; a crowd so insensitive to the suffering of such young men he was left to wonder why he'd risked everything, putting aside his own family.

Jeremiah though had seen this spectacle before, having been at the hanging of Colonel Despard, who by coincidence was also charged with High Treason. He remembered listening to him when he stood upon the scaffold to give a hero's speech, the crowd cheering him on. The atmosphere charged with a menace you could feel, so volatile they would have had Despard down and away if not for so many soldiers. He also remembered it was the brother of one of the men about to hang who had turned evidence, signing his sibling's life away in effect, none of which was filling him with any kind of hope.

Later the same day the noise of someone a little more vocal than the usual occupant was just about to join them. Many knew instantly who, Thomas Bacon was brought through to an overwhelming silence. Jeremiah heard a lot of talk from them, about if it wasn't for the old man they would not be rotting there. While he was left to consider his own position, yet they seemed to accept him; for which he was grateful, but could not help but find bizarre. Bacon was indeed one of them and he a relative stranger. Then even more commotion for Thomas Bacon was led of to be ironed protesting vehemently about it. From what they could hear this new irritation was not something he'd expected. Maybe because of this some mellowed, but Jeremiah watched quietly how Bacon began to win over those who listened. Though what he said was in every case the truth.

*

In South Wingfield and the surrounding areas, the wives of those arrested were not to be ignored. Taking it upon themselves to raise whatever money they could to pay for a defence for their loved ones. Rebecca Weightman had sent word around each village for them to meet and discuss matters, for time was pressing. The meeting was to be in one of the little stone cottages away from prying eyes. There was a lot of care taken, so no one would know such a thing was taking place.

Standing before them, Rebecca held within an inner steel, that is rarely seen, except in times of the worst adversity. Wrought with emotion and a determination to succeed despite any that might speak against her, she looked about the gathering.

It was this manner that impressed Jeremiah when George had introduced her as though royalty, appreciating it all with a quiet humour.

She was a strong woman with handsome features, holding a presence many could not match, holding her family together now by cleaning for Hugh Wolstenholme, the Pentrich curate.

Taking a breath Rebecca Weightman went to the point like a kingfisher dives into a pond, no flowery words or introduction required. "I will not sleep in a comfortable bed while my husband, who's tried for me, for all of us, to have a better life

———

lies ironed on a cold stone floor."

A general murmuring went around, but no one spoke. Angered by that her eyes devoured them. "I would sooner sell all I have for their defence, than lie easy in my bed while they suffer God knows what."

Some nodded, but Mrs. Weightman wanted more than mere appreciation, she wanted everything they had.

A young blonde woman sprang from her chair, emboldened by this passionate address. "I would sell everything I own to bring them home without a rope about their neck, that is the truth." Tears welling within eyes that shone like diamonds in the twilight of an already poor abode; that would in the near future be without a stick of furniture to sit on.

An older woman leant forward in her chair, sighing so deep the room fell quiet in an instant. All now intent on what she had to say, for her husband Isaac had good standing in the village, being a Methodist preacher. Greying hair was held tight under a white bonnet, a pristine apron on her lap, appeared as if to glow within the darkening room, the worry she endured written more eloquently upon her face than any words could tell. Wringing her hands in an unconscious effort to relieve some small measure of distress. A lass no more than twelve, crossed the room to sit beside her, placing her hand upon her lap.

The words pulled from her. "Mrs. Weightman, speaks the truth, and we would be advised to listen. I need no bed since that night I watch daylight flood the window like an imposter, to watch it leave, not knowing what help I may be." Looking earnestly

toward Rebecca Weightman. "My furniture is there to sell and I

can only hope it pays for proper men to speak for them, then it

would be worth every farthing we may get."

After Mrs. Ludlam addressed the meeting, it was agreed by

everyone inside the room, they would sell everything they owned.

Many went much further, standing out in all weathers in

Nottingham and all the busy market towns in Derbyshire, asking

for any help people could give to save their menfolk. It was a

valiant effort and when they could get no more, it was Hugh

Wolstenholme, who took the money to those who dealt with it.

Securing lawyers by their efforts, one-stepped forward many

considered the best in the land for such work. A Mr. Thomas

Denman, who had defended men brought to trial on claims of

Luddism, managing to get them off without conviction. The

women were much heartened when they heard and a little hope

began to pulse their veins. The lead counsel was a Mr. John Cross,

which was all they could find out, pleased at least they had proper

counsel and all they could do now was wait and hope.

Unknown to them or those in prison Mr. Cross the leading

counsel, was not considered by some to be the right man to fight

the case. Thomas Denman, though, had impressed everyone, on

finding Brandreth had been on parish relief, decided not to charge

any fee at all to represent them.

Some time later the women gathered when George Booth, one of

the young men hung for firing the hayricks was to be given a fitting burial by the Pentrich curate. Hugh Wolstenholme had hidden George and others after the march and even managed to get him away to Sheffield, only for him to be found some time later and brought back to Derby gaol.

This mark of respect to the lad, though, was too much for William Jeffery Lockett the Crown Solicitor, who was not a man to let things lie, so sent an application to the Home Secretary for Wolstenholme's arrest. Henry Hobhouse was then Under Secretary and dealt this; Henry's brother being John Cam Hobhouse, who later became a radical M.P. supporting the call for male suffrage and a close friend of Lord Byron, for some reason this arrest was never actioned.

*

Jeremiah was now spending his time sucking on a small clay pipe and keeping his own counsel, pondering who deserved respect and maybe who did not. Stevens the leader of the Nottingham Committee had waited along with a number of men on the Forest for the Derby men to come through. Knowing now that John Holmes had accused the London delegate, of being an informer two days before they marched, and that Holmes was not the only one to have their doubts. Leaving him to wonder why Stevens had not sent word that things might be upon the turn? Who would have thought Holmes would have a better heart and more sense than the rest? By the look of him no one would consider him the sanest.

He'd heard from the men in Derby gaol that Stevens was still

151

calling for them to come up while he sat drinking in an inn at Nuthall. This after sending the message back through George Weightman that Nottingham was taken; the soldiers would not come from the barracks, bring the men up. With no support having arrived from the north and his own numbers lower than expected, what was he thinking? The only thing in their favour was that many waited in the Market Square, only to return to their homes, after a few disturbances and a number of arrests.

Then there was the information from the villagers of Eastwood, who hurried over to them in a state of panic when they arrived. Stating that a magistrate had ridden through telling them he was going to the barracks, to alert the infantry. The magistrate must have ridden along the very same road Stevens was on at that time, so why hadn't he stopped him? Surely, Stevens realised whatever the magistrate was about, it did not bode well for them.

Yet William Stevens was a man who claimed to be willing to stake his life and take life if it was needed, which appeared nothing but idle posturing now. Stevens would not have been alone or without firearms, so the magistrate should have been easily contained.

If the Derbyshire army had managed to arrive in the Market Square, would Nottingham have risen, very likely, many waited there, however, Stevens did not stop him and nothing could change what happened now. Through all of it, however, Jeremiah just thought him to be of poor judgment with just enough ability to save himself and those with him, which it turned out, was in fact a better achievement than he had managed.

The protestations of Thomas Bacon began to strike a different chord, he could not join them on account of a warrant out for his arrest, it had no meaning, it did not matter in the slightest. If they were caught, he'd have much more to worry over. If successful it would have mattered even less. Yet Bacon had waited thirty years for this. Jeremiah smiled to himself maybe he should have put him on the pony instead of George. That was the only sane reason he could not join them, him being sixty odd years of age. It was apparent Bacon sensed things were turning and turned off at the last moment. The best he could think; was that Thomas Bacon had hoped that he was wrong. He wondered now if Bacon had been in charge of the Nottingham Committee would he have let this march go ahead or not, but Thomas Bacon was not in charge and William Stevens was. Both had much the same effect, but William Stevens had, however, managed to turn up with no impact whatsoever.

If Thomas Bacon did as Jeremiah now considered, think things were upon the turn, why had he allowed his kin to go? Surely, he would have alerted George to this. George being Thomas Bacon's nephew, the landlady of The White Horse was Thomas Bacon's sister and a woman of strong opinions like her brother. None of it mattered now, and he spoke to no one of his thoughts, keeping this counsel to himself.

It was now Bacon began declaring long and loud that it was plain William Oliver had built this with the backing of the government, so they could be seen to be strong in rooting out those intent upon reform, all of which was true.

Jeremiah knew from talk going around he was not alone in this consideration, and Bacon was beginning to deflect the blame.

Although Jeremiah was desperate for change, would he have led this march if he had known the northern leaders were taken up and talk was the London delegate was a spy? John Holmes so sure that he accused him openly at a meeting on the seventh, two days before they marched and wanted to put an end to him? If it hadn't been for Stevens belief in Oliver it may well have happened.

Would any of them have done this, if William Oliver had not told them everywhere was far more eager than they to get the job done, that they would be letting others down if they did not march?

William Oliver was the instrument that led them into this, knowing everything he told them was a lie. They were just the unlucky recipients of his handiwork. While others it seemed had more consideration for their own neck when the moment came, numbers being far lower than they'd been led to believe, or was that just another lie.

Indeed now the act was played many of the leading radicals were distancing themselves daily from their actions. Henry Hunt valiantly stuck by them, asking if any could offer help, hoping to secure aid for men that listened to every word these radicals had uttered. The answer from some quarters a resounding no; they had damaged their cause instead of helped it, which was a fine thing to say. True these radicals had not openly instigated rebellion, but William Oliver made the case that these same radicals waited upon this action. Truth was they had talked ardently of change, using stronger and stronger language to men suffering the worst extremes of poverty. It was not hard to believe the country was ready, word had been received from other areas in previous weeks, but unfortunately no one had the money to go and check if it held true prior to the event.

William Cobbett, one of the leading radicals had avoided prison for seditious talk by reappearing in America earlier in the year, if only they could have done the same. None of which was filling Jeremiah with any kind of hope.

When the trial was almost upon them, they were warned no one was to mention William Oliver, and if they did it would not go well with them in the eyes of the judge. Many marchers had never met him, so had no idea who he was anyway.

By Jeremiah's own admission in a written statement, he met Oliver after the Whit Monday meeting and it seems likely it was here he was persuaded to undertake the venture. Later when the trial was over and the verdict in; he was heard to mutter in unguarded moments, that if it was not for Oliver he would not have been there.

*

Before the proceedings began the judge ordered that no one was to be allowed to discuss the trial until its conclusion or include anything before the 8th of June. Thus, stifling the press, who may have written about Oliver's, instigation and encouragement, while relaying who he worked for?

Never having been read the riot act, by law most should have been let off with a warning, except for the shooting of Robert Walters, which had all the hallmarks of manslaughter.

Most were energised by their own situation and the preaching's of Thomas Bacon, who unfortunately believed every word William Oliver said. Well, that was until the week before; then his thoughts began to turn. They were also inspired by Jeremiah's rousing address; he could not have tried harder to that end.

Some joined the march because friends or family insisted they fought this repressive government. In reality it mattered little who was to blame, with the exception of William Oliver and those paying him, himself for his belief in the right of what he did or Bacon for his years of preaching, they could only wait for the final act to play.

*

On Thursday the 2nd of September, the prisoners were issued with lists of jurors and prosecution witnesses. The jury being filled with the richest landowners in the area, Right Honourables, and Sirs, while the witnesses against them, included many that had marched, so were turning evidence, possibly with the promise of saving themselves.

Lockett, the Solicitor for the Crown, said he had information on which he could depend, that those who were to serve upon the jury were most respectable, and there would be few challenges.

One name upon the list stood out above the rest, Colonel

Wingfield Halton, the very same man who'd had his hayricks burnt was to sit and decide their fate. Also the two Special Constables who were drinking with them at The White Horse, and the owners of the houses they visited that night. There was no joy in this day for them at all.

It was not until Thursday the twenty fifth of September the judges began to arrive in Derby. On Friday the men were brought into the courtroom in groups, to have the indictment read against them. It was announced Mr. Robert Bond and Mr. Thomas Wragg were to be their Solicitors with Mr. John Cross and Mr. Thomas Denman their Counsel. The trial would start on the 15th of October, from then on it began to feel like a huge beam of light searched them out every moment that they had.

Jeremiah was brought through to meet Thomas Denman, a magistrate having insisted on being present. He was still ironed, but not enough to stop the decisive walk he always had. Thinking back to following old Tobias out of the inn, he realised then that, that was why the old man walked that way, wondering what he had done to deserve it?

Thomas Denman came round the table and for some reason this did not leave the best impression upon his client. Both Denman and the magistrate were expensively dressed as if they were going to a later appointment, with high collared double-breasted jackets, cut high above the waist and fancy shirts. A fashion that suited Denman, but did nothing for the magistrate, and to accentuate the point he wore a gaudy, silk embroidered waistcoat underneath the jacket, which all seemed a little out of place.

Denman was a tall striking man, not without a little attitude, while the magistrate, looked like a suckling pig, sitting to one side, giving the impression he was slightly bored.

Reading out a few of the statements against his client, Denman asked if he had anything to say?

His client shrugged, considering this meeting little more than a charade, much like the trial. At which his counsel paced a moment and tried again. "Mr. Brandreth this is your chance to tell me your truth, how you see what happened and from there I can present a case."

Jeremiah relented in his way, which was not exactly what his counsel wanted. "I am a skilled man, seven years apprentice to my craft, yet my family live next to starvation, along with thousands more." Casting a sideways glance at the magistrate. "The merchants and their Truck system, designed to chain folk to poverty. Not once do they deal fairly or reduce what is asked; yet it is plain those who work under this system suffer distress, while they grow rich upon it. Not once. Indeed, they ask for more, like some ill-bred child that knows no boundaries. And you ask why I am here?" Their roles appeared reversed.

Denman looked shocked by this address, but his client wasn't done.

Turning on the magistrate with a look of vitriolic glee. "How does your money come, for you look well upon it, if such a state can be considered so? Framework knitters, miners, those that

———

labour?" Starting to laugh when the magistrate began to show a deeper colour. "There's more than a few the same for one reason or t'other."

The magistrate felt himself more than a match for the pauper, flicking a piece of thread from his trousers. "Someone better presented than your self no doubt," shaking, but trying to hold his anger.

The pauper smiled, his face grey with dirt, much like his clothes, his hair unkempt, unshaven, but there was something within, for all their fine clothes airs and graces, neither man would ever match.

Thomas Denman guessed that more was coming.

"Aye she is as lovely as her station allows, being pregnant. Tis' exercise you need, the mines should put you right, if you could but get inside 'um. And here before us, is gluttony in privilege."

Enraged the magistrate raised himself with some difficulty. "How dare you?" His trousers pulling under the gor-belly that went before him. Even more irritated when it highlighted his appraisal. "There is a reason you are here," his face the colour of a ripened apple.

Jeremiahs picture now complete. "Taking great delight in his discomfort, he looked at him with a calm that belied the situation. "Aye, because the likes a' you have no boundary to their greed," that calm turning to anger.

Looking slightly under-dressed, his trouser underneath his Stomach, the magistrate scuttled from the room trying to adjust his clothing, but not before sending a withering glance toward Thomas Denman, who followed, attempting to assuage his feelings slightly stunned.

Jeremiah allowed himself a smile, 'til Denman strode back into the holding cell somewhat irritated, placing his hands either side of the table opposite. "You realise of course you may have delivered yourself a blow I cannot rectify."

The simmering anger resurfaced and he was in no mood to relent. "*I need not care whether I live or die, for there are no 'Derbyshire Ribs' now.*" {6} "The man is no more than a slug, feeding off the sweat of others, dress him in all the fancy clothes you like, but that is what you'll find beneath."

Collecting up his papers having written absolutely nothing, Denman issued from the room without another word, wondering what his client was talking about. He was left to consider, had this man the desire or opportunity he would have made a very able leading counsel. Finding out later that the 'Derbyshire Rib' was the work Jeremiah produced and with no employment to be found anywhere, had nothing to keep his family from the poverty they endured.

To add to these concerns, that evening on meeting with leading counsel, he was to learn that Mr. Cross had asked for his fee upfront, or would not take the case. Believing he would not get paid after the event. Which meant they could not afford the legal fees to gain witnesses. Incensed by this and that their lives appeared to matter so little, why in God's name had he taken the case, unable to hold onto his annoyance. "Why would you do this, surely you knew their station in life?"

Cross didn't appear the least bit ruffled. "It is all resolved. William Oliver will not be mentioned, as far as I am aware I do not think Brandreth ever met him, so will be called first and is likely to feel the full measure of the law." He smiled.

"And Thomas Bacon?" Denman bristled, not just because Cross showed no thought at all towards the defendants, but because his own position was deemed so insignificant.

"He will be called sometime later, well down the pecking order so to speak. The man cannot be trusted to keep quiet about Oliver."

It appeared The Nottingham Captain's fate was sealed before he ever stepped into court, along with those with him. Standing silent a moment Denman took in the implications of what was said saying nothing more.

When the men were told Thomas Bacon was not first into court that it was their Captain, everyone felt the ground shifting beneath them. Heartened, as they were to have proper counsel, it did not seem right to them. The men knew whom they considered the prime motivator, though, Jeremiah would be amongst the number, his would not be the first name upon the sheet if they had written it. They had never met William Oliver, however, and if any deserved a slice of justice, was there ever a better subject.

The date was set, on learning he was to be called first Jeremiah showed no emotion. To the outside observer it appeared he viewed it all like a play. Mapping out the only course he could take with honour and didn't feel the need to comment on it.

William Turner went across to him, knowing this was not the best of signs. "It seems strange to us they call you first, will you say ought in your defence." Hoping it would hearten him a little, to know the men did not consider it right, though he was next before the jury.

Jeremiah smiled and understood, he sat in the exercise yard his back against the wall, William dropping down beside him. "I will leave it to those paid for it. Anyhow, what can I say?" He shrugged. "I feel no different, we were not wrong. It is they who are wrong, treating folk less than animals." Glancing at William, then back to the yard floor. "Should I say, if those that gave their word had joined us on that night, maybe I would sit in judgment and those that judge would lie here upon this floor in chains?" He shrugged, giving a small but bitter snort of laughter. "If I had known no one would join us from the north; and you asked me that very question, would I have marched? I do not know the answer? I might have considered it foolhardy and known it would come to naught?" Saying no more, just staring before him.

William swallowed, knowing with these statements Jeremiah had fervently believed what he'd been told. He was not part of any duplicity that trapped the Derbyshire men, his heart was heavier for that knowledge. His only lies amounted to telling them they would get, rum, beer, beaf and on their arrival in Nottingham and once there it would be nothing but a jaunt of pleasure. As it happened, they'd not done too badly for the beer, with the inns they'd stopped at. William afforded himself a smile at the thought, remembering how Jeremiah stood fast beside him, urging them twice to make a stand and hold while the Dragoons raced full speed towards them, sabre's drawn The thought crossed William's mind, would they have been better to have stood there upon that day than this?

*

The days wore on, with all the men much more anxious than before, knowing what conviction might bring.

Throughout this time Jeremiah made a little workbag out of materials he had, time went on and it saddened him to see it dirty, heartening himself with the thought that it could wash. Spending his time sewing flowers of different colours on it, considering Ann might have it for a keepsake. Even if he didn't hang, he was certain he would never see his family again, but kept these thoughts to himself.

The closer the trial came, there was but one place they could turn, Jeremiah included, for he was a committed Baptist, finding it gave him the courage to face what might be. For even a sinner such as he could enter the kingdom of heaven through the redeeming blood of Christ. This, though, did not mean he was about to spill his secrets to the chaplain, who constantly badgered him for information on his family or anything that he had done. To which his reply was always curt, he did not wish to make any statements on such matters.

Isaac Ludlam was now recounting prayers day and night many tried to lift his spirits. His only solace was found in prayer and a visit from his family and in the situation, who could say that he was wrong?

A sense of anticipation could be felt throughout Derby in the days before the trial, hundreds of jurors and nearly the same number of prosecution witnesses, suddenly descended upon the town. It became apparent there was nothing like someone else's desperate predicament, to excite a level of human interest many had never seen before. The event was eagerly awaited by those not involved and was to be reported throughout the country when the verdicts were in. All the inns in Derby were now full, and though William Oliver was not to be mentioned in court; there were those with the firm intention he was not to be forgotten. Knowing the judges would attend church just before the trial, upon the church walls the words were written large. *"Jurymen Remember Oliver."* [7]

When Jeremiah was called to go into court still heavily ironed, as many as could get to him wished him well. He was separated from them, but not before George Weightman came to wring his hand. "I wish you good fortune Captain." It was the first time he had ever seemed less than his usual self.

Jeremiah smiled and nodded, but said nothing. Once in court, he did not feel a lift in spirits looking at the jury, their clothing warned him of their position in life. The court was full in fact they were having trouble keeping folk out. The only people of his

station in life were the folk that sat behind him, to view
proceedings.

He listened to Sir Samuel Shepard the Attorney General, when
opening the prosecution's case. Announcing that it mattered little
how many were assembled, it only mattered that they were intent
upon overthrowing the government and that he, Jeremiah
Brandreth, was the leader of that force. Labouring long on the
details of Robert Walters' death, although, Jeremiah Brandreth was
not being tried upon that charge, only on the charge of High
Treason.

The first witness was called and sure enough it was Anthony
Martin, one of the Special Constables who'd listened to their talk
at The White Horse. Then came the second, Shirley Astbury, with
the same sort of questions asked. Jeremiah smiled to himself when
both were asked, if as Special Constables and on hearing that
rebellion was planned, when did they go to the magistrate and
alert the authorities? Both replied that they told no one, they were
too afraid, the landlady had threatened to shove them up the
chimney, at which a ripple of amusement went around the
courtroom. Another witness told the packed court that they
rapped upon his door and stated they were going to Nottingham,
and thousands would meet them there with a band of music.

More sniggering from behind, but the look upon the faces of the
jury hadn't changed at all.

Others appeared, some having marched without coercion,
extricating themselves from prosecution by giving evidence

against their comrades. Then Thomas Turner, a relative of William yet to have his trial, recounted the death of Robert Walters' at Mrs. Hepworth's house.

Jeremiah could not bring himself to even look at him, fixing his gaze upon the floor in front. Having stated to Thomas Denman that he was alone at the back of the house when the incident occurred, so how could anyone else know what had happened.

Though, Thomas Denman was impressed with Brandreth's character he would maintain that he was duped into this through the lies of others and it was a riot, nothing more. There was short mention of his despair at being on parish relief, that he had a young family to provide for, it passed as if unsaid. Nor did Denman make much of the fact he had not allowed the men under his command to `Draw the Badger.' A term used for getting Colonel Wingfield Halton out of his house to shoot him, in reprisal for the lads that at the time of the rising were waiting to be hung, which in effect had saved his life. Or given ample opportunity, Brandreth did nothing to George Goodwin, the manager of Butterley Ironworks, when he could quite easily have shot him, Goodwin having come amongst them to dissuade them from their course.

Nothing much was mentioned that he never even attempted an attack upon the place, letting George Goodwin walk back inside the Ironworks without harming a hair upon his head. It was mentioned, but not given a thorough airing, 'though why Thomas Denman did not play upon these things more seemed odd. Maybe

Mr. Denman was doing a little political manoeuvring of his own, ending up as Lord Chief Justice in the years that followed, after his defence of Queen Charlotte. Indeed, those that knew the story might wonder whose side Brandreth's defence was on. Some said Brandreth was impulsive and hotheaded, but none of these things seem that. Maybe he followed the orders he was given too strictly, but having a military background, he would. By his own admission to George Weightman while in prison, he had been a Luddite and he followed their tactics throughout. Indeed many that marched were framework knitters with those connections, and most could read and write, which was unusual for the time.

The fact their leading counsel denied them the opportunity of having witnesses for their defence, left Henry Hunt, who sat upon the front row at the trial, to wonder exactly how Cross had been picked to defend them in the first place.

At the summing up Jeremiah was asked if he had anything to say in his defence. Without moving an inch he said, *"I leave it to my counsel."* {8} Looking before him as he had throughout the trial, listening to their talk go this way and that.

The days blended into one and on the 18th of October 1817, at five past ten the Jury went out to decide Jeremiah Brandreth's fate. It took them all of twenty-five minutes to come to a decision, returning a verdict of guilty of High Treason.

Jeremiah looked about him, no matter how expected this news carried the capacity to shock. He felt himself swallow becoming dizzy, continuing to stare in front of him unable to focus properly, thinking only of Ann and how she would take this news.

The hope they would receive the same leniency, as those in Yorkshire had been slim, and now they had the answer. He was completely unaware of what was happening around him, that the courtroom was being forcibly emptied. People came asking different things, he had little idea what. A glass of warm spiced wine was put into his hands and Jeremiah gave an awkward little bow, "Thank ye, kindly," the fuss unnoticed. Someone fetched his sefton pipe, which was dirty, like the bag he'd made, he gave another bow receiving it, his thoughts coming back to him while he puffed upon it.

From the seats behind he heard a woman's voice.

"Jeremiah, 'tis Rose."

Half turning, yet in his mind he looked at Ann.

Rose pushed a parcel across to him; he was still handcuffed to the goaler, Mr. Eaton.

"Thank ye, most kindly." How he missed hearing a woman's voice.

"God have mercy on you Jeremiah."

Remembering her, and her kindness he gave the sort of smile when you're not sure how to be and tried to stuff the sandwiches into his hat to carry them. There were so many he was advised to hold them by the gaoler and wrapped them in a scarf instead. Mutely he waited for the escort to take him from court, he had not written to Ann since his arrest, he must write now, not the words he would have wanted. Asking the Chaplain if it were possible.

He smiled and nodded. "Indeed, I will fetch everything, you can do it immediately." Hurrying away.

While waiting for his return Jeremiah was taken from court to the little chapel, trying not to let his emotions better him.

The chaplain was soon back, handing the paper to him. "Do you wish me to pray with you?"

"I would be most grateful for it. Thank ye." Looking at the paper.

The chaplain sat on the pew in front, a little to one side looking before him while Jeremiah wrote.

Derby Gaol 18th October 1817.

My dear Beloved wife,   At last I thought it my duty to write a few lines to you, which I am sure will affect you much, to inform you of my dreadful situation; but I hope God will be your friend — and if you will by prayer appeal to God you will undoubtedly find great consolation and relief from your distress, and as a husband and father let me entreat you, that you will act a motherly part to the poor fatherless children and bring them up in the fear of God….And I pray to God may this fatal stroke be joy that all who belong to me, instead of sorrow.

*My dear, you may suppose my feelings are not easily described. My dear wife, it would give me great consolation if I could see you before I depart this life, but my dear, if you are *enceinte I would have you advise with your poor distressed mother in law, whether it would be proper or not; and if she thinks it would not be of serious consequence, I should be* *very glad, but let it be well considered before you come to me and if you do not come, let your father [if he thinks it would not be more than he could bear, as I know he is of a timorous turn] but if neither come, I shall write again, if God permit me. So my beloved wife, I hope you will excuse my short letter at this time. You may inform all friends that God gave me great fortitude to bear up my spirits on trial. So I hope the blessings of God be with you all, and most especially with you and our little babes.*

Your most affectionate husband.
Jeremiah Brandreth. [9]

Folding the paper, he placed his hand upon it for a moment, then looked to the chaplain, who stood and led him in the Lord's prayer. He was transferred back into the exercise yard, the prisoners circling to hear his news, it was just past twelve.

George Weightman hurried over, he did not ask, but his eyes were fixed on Jeremiah, who seemed to have momentarily lost his usual composure. No one dared to speak, but every man waited upon the answer. Looking before him, Jeremiah lifted his head and regaining the same stoic calm, looking at no one in particular, "Guilty."

There was a gasp, no one spoke; William Turner put his hand upon his shoulder. In a surreal moment, of unprecedented calm, remembering the sandwiches, he offered them about. Truth was since his arrival in prison he'd not been able to stomach much, now the pangs of hunger left him altogether. This generosity did not hearten them any, a silence overtaking the anticipation they felt moments ago. Knowing they were not to be treated like those in Yorkshire and let off with a warning.

Jeremiah was still coming to terms with his fate, although sentence was not passed; he was now certain it would be the very worst they could throw at him. All he could think of was Ann and the family he loved so much? Yet every man deserved more than the abject poverty his family suffered, he sat trying to steel himself against what he now must face, though he had always known if things went adrift how it would turn, he had prayed it might be different. Having put his faith in the counsel of others, and like the rest been taken in by one working for the government; who had no more thought for their lives, than the weight within his pocket.

He had hoped those he led might be allowed back to their family, now those hopes were all receding like the sea disappears into the sand, a myriad of feelings juggled for position, but always in his heart lay the knowledge, he was not wrong.

Being used to walking long distances, it was his only solace now and had been since his imprisonment, so started pacing up and down the yard.

The prisoners who were ironed took his verdict badly and sat staring before them saying naught, all except for Isaac, who was praying.

Jeremiah heard this when he passed and stopped to sit beside him. "Isaac, It is my hope the rest may get a lesser sentence," there was a smile but no reply. Jeremiah was left to reflect and pray that Isaac found a great deal of comfort from his prayers.

Wondering how many more they would see fit to convict, hoping he would be the only one. If they needed an example surely that would be enough.

Sitting there in silence remembering the letter he had written, the joy it would be to see Ann now. When everything is stripped away the sudden wonder of someone so beloved, just the sight of them, even if they could not touch, would be a relief. Knowing prisoners usually met their visitors by looking through a hatch, and Ann might be allowed no closer.

Treasured remembrances came to comfort to him, the days they walked in the sun, happy carefree days came to him. When he sat by the River Idle on the village green, with Sal and Bill, laughing over some stupid thing someone had done.

Recalling how worried he had been when Elizabeth was born. How relieved he was when he knew they were both well, it was all he'd wanted, knowing how many mothers died in childbirth. 'Though he never said to anyone, he had prayed so many times then. Smiling on recalling Ann's delight at holding the babe and showing her to him, it was a moment in his life that could not be matched. Then Timothy's appearance, Ann delighted to have given him one of each, arriving with a head full of black curls, too everyone's amusement. Jeremiah's uncle slapping him upon the back, "tis a wonder he didn't come out wearing thee top hat lad," which started them off in 'The Frameworkers', the inn turning into one huge celebration. Their laughter going round the crowded alehouse, where they'd snuck off to wet the baby's head, Ann's father with them. Disappearing when all the women arrived at Bedlam Court to coo over the new babe, with mountains of little knitted gifts, Ann being the best mother a child could want.

In his mind he was stood inside the church, waiting for the loveliest girl in the town to come and stand beside him, pledging herself to him. Turning when she walked into the church, he saw in his mind's eye Bill and Sally grinning at him, his uncle whispering that he had the ring. Looking at Ann, the sight of her taking his words away and realised now he'd never said the things he meant too. Watching as she walked towards him down the aisle, her chestnut hair all curled and waved, a circle of flowers within it, those stunning hazel eyes casting about to find those she loved. The scent of the flowers lifting through that lovely church, picked specially that morning from her father's garden.

How proud he felt when Ann stood there beside him to take her vows, for some strange reason he could not even now recall his own, remembering how her voice trembling and how he'd smiled to give her courage. Her hand reaching for his before she should, giggling when she realised her mistake, he had held it tight, never wanting to let go, if only he'd kept to that.

William Turner looked at Isaac, then sat beside Jeremiah, a silent gesture of support and Jeremiah grateful for it. Deep in their different memories, Jeremiah knowing his could never to be repeated. Bitter thoughts came to him, how they had been left to suffer the consequences; by those that could have warned them things were turning. Nevertheless, he was not sorry, only sorry the northern leaders were taken up, so did not march.

He'd heard there'd been some disturbance in Huddersfield; other places that were to rise appeared to have aborted. Before they tried those in Huddersfield, however, the Leeds Mercury had exposed the role of William Oliver. The jury therefore, decided upon a verdict of not guilty, a direct result of his incitement. Given that warning, the government now were far more devious.

Many he knew had turned allegiance to save themselves, in his heart he did not feel the need to blame them, with the exception of those that lied to do it. They would live to fight or not another day, but he would die for something he believed in, for him there was no other choice.

There were those who fought to save the marchers, spilling their thoughts on the subject to any newspaper that would print it. Incensed at the underhand behaviour of the government, but this did not get through to the jury in any way at all. Henry Hunt again angered by leading counsel Cross when he called William Cobett's writings, "malignant and ignorant,"[10] when conducting his speeches in court.   While most who knew of Oliver's role were repulsed by this Agent Provocateur who actively encouraged the rebellion. Telling them at a meeting at the Three Salmons they would be letting their country down if they did not march, for the rest waited on their actions. This was said again the next day at the meeting Jeremiah attended, until then he had not been sure enough to lead it. It was at this meeting Oliver made a point of speaking to him; making him feel he would be the lesser man for not having the resolve needed. That seventy thousand in London waited upon Nottingham being secure before they dared to rise. Saying over and over, that the leading radicals were waiting so they could finally help the thousands suffering. Oh! He had twisted the knife and found the soul within the man. Only then did Jeremiah truly believe he had no other choice, throwing his life away for a devious liar and a traitor to reform, paid in a ransom of blood the exchange for their lives.

Knowing his own trial was soon upon him William was unable to sit for long, so took to walking the yard again considering his life, thinking of the girl he'd hoped would share it; that was until she found someone else for the position. Never having mentioned his intentions; he wondered now if he had; would it have made a difference? It was the reason he'd taken the King's shilling, being very young at the time, spending many years and campaigns within the ranks. Knowing he could never stomach watching the happy couple going about their lives, so decided to serve his King instead. In two days time he would face the jury and could only hope he would have better fortune than his Captain.

William hadn't the easy life Jeremiah had within the army; he had seen active service time and time again. Having returned from these campaigns to find life much harder than expected, he'd attended Hampden Club meetings with Thomas Bacon and listened to him preaching. Busying him self by building a home for his parents throughout this time, knowing it would stand for years. Wanting to put his mind to something he could look on and appreciate in the years to come, never realising he had less time than most to do it.

George Weightman joined him, both standing now to watch Brandreth get up and start pacing up and down the yard like every other day. Nodding in his direction. "He seems to be taking the news better than I'd a thought any man might."

"He is made of something other." William let out a sigh.

"I have never known you fear anything my friend." Feeling the anxiety in William's voice.

Considering his years in the ranks, he smiled. "If I get the same," looking toward the Captain, "I am not sure how I will face it. Though I have seen death many times and delivered it in service of the King and the course of my duty, but never caged, with the certainty that it awaits me. At least when you serve your country, you have a chance of winning, it does not seem that way this time." Suddenly agitated. "How can we be charged with High Treason, for the love of God!" He laughed, his anger calming as suddenly as it came.

George shook his head wanting to keep up his spirits. "Surely it will be enough to make an example of our Captain, there is no need for more. I am certain you will have better fortune. It is not what we would want I know, but my guess is they will send us to other lands, an' 'tis better than the hangman. I have heard if you do what is asked of you, you may gain your freedom or have it granted on arrival, but 'tis like the desert for the heat."

William was not convinced. "You think it likely? You do not think we are ironed like the Captain, so are likely to receive the same verdict?"

"I cannot see a point to it." George looked somewhat disheartened William did not agree and withdrew into a silence of his own.

Leaving William to pondered what was said. They were both ironed like their Captain, surely it meant they were likely to receive the same penalty, but George was always one to seek out the best outcome of any given situation.

After the Captain's verdict and from what he knew had been said at his trial, William began to feel there was no one they could trust, not even those paid for it. Knowing many had turned evidence; but given the choice he supposed many would.

They sat in silence staring before them, William feeling no better for George's company, which was unusual. Pondering how his family would take whatever was to come. Feeling he had let them down, because he was the one who made certain they had everything they needed, and if this verdict went against him he could not bring himself to think what it would mean for them. Deciding he must write, knowing the Captain had done so and it seemed appropriate.

William's trial came and went in much the same manner; only now both defence lawyers claimed William had been manipulated by Brandreth's clever words and malign influence. To add insult to injury Denman read out a long quote from Lord Byron's poem, The Corsair, likening their Captain to Conrad, the leader of a band of pirates, saying he had a decisiveness and manner about him that could easily sway others to his purpose.

What Jeremiah thought on learning this he never said, just gave a chagrined snort of laughter when he heard.

Truth was, they were roused by Jeremiah's inspired speeches, for he believed it to be true. However, if he never appeared before them, they would still have marched with William leading in all probability, roused by Thomas Bacon and their own circumstance.

Some like Brandreth suffered unemployment and saw starvation staring back. Their bravery was due to a strong sense of what they thought right, in response to what they saw happening around them. The memory of the young men they'd watched hang, still roused the same anger they had felt when they joined the march all those weeks ago.

When Brandreth came to them, however, it is true they could not have wanted for a more driven or courageous leader.

*

Elizabeth hurried into the back room, looking anxiously at George, to place a letter upon the table beside her daughter.

Ann gazed a moment at the handwriting and smiled, then stood quite suddenly to announce that she would go to Mrs. Stones and ask if she would read the letter for her. Returning together before reading, to sit in the backyard upon an upturned tub in the drizzle.

Mrs. Stones was an educated woman knowing how to read and write, who used to have a drapery business years ago, and thought it best for Ann to have her family around her when this news was delivered. Still doing the odd order now and then for folk with enough money to require it, now of course there weren't so many in that position. Each wrapping a shawl around them to combat the drizzle, reading the letter in a quiet resigned manner, for she could only guess this news would not be good; afterwards Ann said nothing, just sat staring at the wall as if she hadn't heard; wearing an unbecoming shade of grey, the shawl slipping from her shoulders.

Mrs. Stones placed her hand upon Ann's arm. "I am so sorry it's come to this, my dear." Getting to her feet she bent to give Ann a gentle hug, but after looking at her, thought the better of it. Hurrying into the house to fetch Elizabeth, for Ann wasn't listening. Leaving when Elizabeth raced into the little yard to kneel before her daughter in the dirt, trying to comfort her.

The next day Ann had recovered herself enough to go and thank Mrs. Stones, taking some of her fathers flowers with her and ask a further favour, if she would write a letter that she might send to Jeremiah.

"Of course, I was just about to come across, to see if you intended to write back." She smiled and did no more than start upon it.

To   Jeremiah Brandreth

alias, The Nottingham Captain

alias, John Coke

Sutton Oct 26th 1817

*I received your unwelcome letter [or rather the unwelcome news it
contains] on the 25th. And it is in vain for me to attempt to describe my
feelings on the arrival of such unwelcome tidings it contains. I leave you
to judge my feelings yet distressing as my situation is it is nothing in
comparison to yours [I mean as to the situation I am left in] but I shall
forbear saying much at this time as I intend if God permits to see you in
the course of one week. If I can by any means find conveyance in the
meantime. I hope that that God which is more merciful than Man will
give you comfort and consolation and if you have [as is the general
opinion] been drawn by that Wretch Oliver forgive him and leave him to
God and his own conscience, that God who will give to every man his
reward I though when I call him a man I scarce think him so, though in
the shape of one.*

*O that I could atone for all and save your life. Praying that God will
be with you to strengthen you and comfort you [and should you suffer]
bring you through Christ to Eternal Glory which is the prayer of your
unhappy wife.*

Ann Brandreth.[11]

Nothing Ann's family said could now dissuade her from her course, and two days later she set out at first light, armed with a few sandwiches and a small flask of water. The weather being good, with a few stops upon the way, though it was the best part of twenty miles, just past mid-day Ann arrived in Derby.

Like Jeremiah, Ann liked to walk and today at least there was only the one child she was carrying. She sat on a low wall to give her feet a rest, and the enormity of her visit began to hit anew.

The keys rattled against the door, Mr. Eaton, the gaoler appeared within the doorway to announce to Jeremiah that he had a visitor.

His heart leapt into his throat at the thought of seeing Ann, it was not the way he wanted it for he looked so dirty and disheveled. Having refused to shave before the trial, saying he would go to the gallows like it and had no intention of changing his mind. Hurrying into the holding room not expecting to see her there. Mr. Eaton moved into the furthest corner, out of the way uninterested.

Jeremiah stood a moment gazing at her, seeing how the growing child had made her blossom, for pregnancy always suited Ann.

Just one step towards him, though, no one else would notice, he saw the smile within her eyes and felt the hurt he saw there.

The gaoler, realising her condition hurried towards her with a chair, and went back to whatever he was doing in the corner.

Allowing Jeremiah to sit opposite, the irons not allowing him much movement. Just for a moment he was miles away from the place he now resided. Then saw her eyes and knew that she was struggling, dragging her back with no one else the wiser. "Remember how we danced upon the Green, what we talked about that night, remember now." Watching her swallow to look down a moment, then take her lead from what he'd said.

Trying to dislodge the impact of seeing him in chains, looking so very ill and wasted, she could not help but think he'd never make it to the gallows. Holding onto every scrap of resilience she could muster. Turning her mind from what she saw, reminding herself of what they'd said, each to the other when they sat upon the bed at Bedlam Court, all those months ago. Steeling herself to think only of her children. "Surely it is not true, what they are saying?" Trembling like a leaf caught in the breeze and yet she sat so very upright.

There was a slight nod of approval from him. "It matters little now." Closing his eyes for just a second, relieved she had not forgotten how she should distance herself from what he'd done.

"And the map?"

He shrugged. "It is of no importance now." Wanting to hold her just the once, instead he was holding his emotions, but had never found it quite so hard to do as this. He must not implicate her in any way, knowing they were not averse to hanging women for lesser charges than High Treason. Remembering a young woman not yet twenty, they'd hung for handing out looted potatoes from the back of an old cart, to help those desperate for food. He would protect her still the only way he could. "I am so pleased to see you Ann, how did you travel?"

Ann smiled. "The usual way."

"You walked." Sighing resignedly. " I...." Say nothing more, swallowing. "How are the children, kiss them for me, we will meet again one day, have faith Ann?" There was the slightest suggestion of a smile and yet his eyes seemed very distant.

It took a while for her to answer. "The children are well, I pray with them every day, " stopping a moment, "and for you...." unable to go on, a silence fell between them. Yet no one else would ever notice that her heart was bleeding there.

He saw; he heard it breaking, "I do not fear what is before me and I have faith that we will meet again one day, in a better place than this. Bring the children up in the fear of God and let their world and yours be one of joy, not sorrow." Looking deep into her eyes he saw her heart just lying there.

It seemed to her she'd only been there moments when the gaoler's wife came in breaking the silence to bringing a small collection to her, so she might get the coach home instead of walking, after learning Ann had walked all the way knowing the condition she was in, and something for the children.

Accepting it, Ann thanked them.

Jeremiah was certain it was never destined for the coachman's pocket.

Ann felt her hands shake more violently, realising this visit was coming to a close; it became so very hard for her to speak. Inside her head she felt that she was screaming, screaming at a world that didn't care, how strange, that she was sitting as if waiting for a coach, she had no intention of ever taking, none of it felt real. Wanting to hold him in her arms and make them prize her fingers from him. Jeremiah would never give them the satisfaction; they were being watched so she would hold herself until she fell.

In a daze she found herself walking from a hideous red brick building never turning, she couldn't or she would break into a thousand little pieces.

It wasn't until she reached the outskirts of that town; she found a quiet place to cry. Yet when she sat upon the grass there were no tears, only a numbing emptiness that swallowed every thought she had. After sitting stunned a while she picked herself up to find every step became a living nightmare, walking from where she longed to be. Beside the man that made her life complete, though she would never say, because she loved her children so, she felt her life was ending also, so she would live for her babes alone.

Jeremiah rose slowly from the chair to watch her just a second longer; 'til she was lost from view. The gaoler didn't appear to object and let him stand and watch her leave, returning him to the cell that was little more than a passage without a word, the Nottingham Captain lost in thoughts all his own.

*

William's trial concluded and contrary to the feelings of revulsion throughout the country at the devious methods of the government, the jury gave the verdict, guilty of High Treason.

William complained bitterly of perjury amongst those that

turned evidence, many having walked without coercion. He was left to reflect, that no one until faced with the rope, would know how they might react if offered the chance to escape it.

He had written to his former commander in Chief, the Duke of York. After fighting for his country and having been a soldier so long he harboured the hope he might intervene on his behalf. The days progressed and hope drifted away.

He wrote to his family, finding it harder than he'd ever imagined, but in this his cousin Joseph Turner helped him. Looking forward to the day they were to visit, dreading it at the same time, what could he say to comfort them; he had no idea. The strange thing was he wished to comfort them, not considering himself. He would face the hangman; his pain would be over, while they would live forever with the thought of him. Nothing; however, could bring him joy except the sight of them.

Isaac Ludlum's trial concluded with the same awful verdict, guilty of High Treason.

A number had better luck and were to be transported to Australia, some having been assured by counsel they would have their freedom once they landed. Finding that was not the case at all when they arrived, it was just another lie. Others received a prison sentence with hard labour, ranging from a few months to two years the conditions in some prisons abysmal.

One group had better fortune to be let off with a warning about their future conduct, standing in court looking about them, not really understanding they were free men once again.

After sentence was pronounced Jeremiah was to share a cell with George Weightman, Isaac Ludlam and William Turner in another, the four having been separated from the other prisoners.

George had been found guilty of High Treason was not yet sentenced, this was after some deliberation, one member of the jury did not want to give that verdict. After a few days with the terror of not knowing what was coming, he had his sentence commuted and was instead to be transported along with his uncle Thomas Bacon to Australia; fourteen men in all received that sentence.

William watched his Captain march up and down the yard there seemed no fear in him; he stood steadfastly by what he had done with no remorse, considering if things had gone to plan many would have died before the night was through.

Knowing Jeremiah, did not feel contrition, how could he? To do so would deny the reason why they marched upon the ninth, and he would never do that. Though he had said if blood was shed whether a freak accident or not it was merit enough to take his own.

In that way William wondered if Jeremiah admitted guilt, or did he consider it only because he led the march? William would never know and decided he would never ask; he had too much to trouble him already.

Jeremiah did not claim to be anything but singularly disposed to reach Nottingham with a force of men, whatever that took. More than once threatening to blow someone's brains out, to get the guns or conscripts needed for their growing army. To say such a thing though, is very different to doing it and if that was his intention he was given ample opportunity.

William continued to stare in front of him at the figure pacing up and down. While pondering if declaring such things were High Treason, many thousands should be hanging.

Jeremiah's speech in the courtroom before sentence was passed perhaps more telling than any. *"Let me address you in the words of our Saviour. If it be possible, let this cup pass from me, let not my will, but your Lordships' be done."* [12]

Placing the burden of what he considered murder back upon them, while resigning himself to show any disposed to watch, how he would face it. Martyring himself in the hope those who had marched may be spared their lives, without any form of contrition he would defy them to the end.

In the days after the trial; however, in unguarded moments he was heard to mutter, *"Oliver has brought me to this. But for Oliver I should not have been here."* [13]

Lord Byron's speech against the Framework Breaking Bill appeared something of a reality five years later.

In the days leading up to his execution the prison Chaplain, a man named Pickering, tried just like every other week to get Jeremiah to confess to all that he'd done, and to the shooting of Robert Walters, to which he replied, *"he had endeavoured to make his peace with God, and he did not see that it was necessary for him to make any statement for the satisfaction of man."* [14]

It was on the 7th of November 1817, at precisely 12. 35 pm, the drop was actioned and Jeremiah Brandreth, William Turner and Isaac Ludlam were delivered into eternity.

*

Some time earlier Ann walked with her children to St. Mary's church surrounded by her family, holding her emotions. The whole town waiting, all except for Bill, who'd gone to Derby with Rueben and Joe Markham to have the last sight in this life of the man he considered his closest friend.

Having told Sal he felt compelled to be there, to support a man who'd fallen victim to a game the government had played, along with those he led. A game they actively provoked with no thought for those within their grasp, who considered they had no other hope but face starvation.

Those who could have shown compassion consoled themselves with trite cover. Their self-absorption carried over into how well they had done, last year's crops had struggled and they the landed gentry, landowners and rich farmers had survived it all. Riding by huddled groups of paupers on their return from church, to hand a few farthings here and there to ease what was left of a conscience. Returning home to feel a sense of fulfillment and decide upon that extra carriage, for they were doing well in spite of everything. The same men that sat upon a jury, to pronounce verdict upon a starving pauper and those who followed him, who'd marched for better times, and the chance to vote, hoping they could help those suffering.

The congregation of St. Mary's, in stark contrast, sat in stoic silence, if you were inclined to listen you could hear them breathe. When the vicar addressed his flock, his voice carried around the lovely church to give comfort to his flock.

Ann saw his smile, in the hope he could guide her through the hour no doubt. The whole town in mourning, for the anger folk felt at what was done could not be washed away, his calming address nothing compared to the singing that resounded about the church at the appointed time, a small act of defiance on this tragic day; wanting to purge the hour from their memory.

Twelve thirty-five, however, would live with Ann from that moment on and nothing could or would remove it. Feeling herself tremble a little when she stood, to walk from her seat to give her own rendition of Lord Byron's poem, with one alteration of her own, a tribute to the man she would forever love.

Worried glances ran about the congregation, fearing Ann may be unable to complete it.

Looking at them once in position she straightened, before nodding to those who looked on in awe, acknowledging their presence. Just as she looked upon her wedding day, but they would never see the girlish giggle and triumphant smile she wore that day.

Turning her gaze toward her daughter, who sat quietly beside her grandmother not sure what all this meant. Timothy standing upon her knee, clinging with tiny hands, eyes fixed upon his mother, just as he had so many months ago at Bedlam Court when his father kissed him there.

Summoning her courage, she began Lord Byron's poem "And Thou Art Dead, As Young And Fair." Like she addressed folk all her life having memorised the lines, her voice carrying around the church like silver bells.

A stunned silence preceded a round of clapping no one had heard inside a church before. One of the older men shouted "Well done lass." Before he was silenced by a withering glance from his embarrassed wife.

Ann returned to her seat, holding her tears, knowing the husband she so loved was now no more, while the vicar stood to lead them all in prayer.

In a moment known only to herself, a silent tear crept from the corner of her eye, to work its way down her cheek and disappear into the folds of the same fawn dress she'd worn the day they met. Sitting beside her mother not really listening to what the vicar said, cherishing her memories; memories of a day they sat beside the River Idle, to watch it run toward the dam.

When the service was over, Ann walked alone to sit beside the water, the fawn dress one small act of remembrance she alone would know.

* enceinte - pregnant

POSTSCRIPT

The trials concluded with three men to be hung, beheaded and quartered. The Prince Regent repealed the quartering that had been ordered. They were Jeremiah Brandreth 31, William Turner 48, and Isaac Ludlam 52.

Fourteen were transported to Australia, never to return. All after never firing a shot at the cavalry that came against them.

Many radicals of what may be considered the lower orders were imprisoned and kept in close confinement, solitary confinement today, the conditions then appalling.

While in prison Jeremiah never shaved, going to the gallows with a beard, it is said he looked disheveled, but lost none of his stoic courage to the last. The final letter from him to Ann was written just before he was executed.

My Beloved wife

This is the morning before I suffer I have sat down to write my last lines to you hoping that my Soul will be shortly be at rest in heaven through the redeeming blood of Christ I feel no fear in passing through the shadow of death to Eternal life. So I hope you will make the promise to God sure to your own soul that we may meet in heaven where every sorrow will cease and all will be joy love and peace.

My beloved I received a letter this morning with a pound note in it which I leave for you in the Gaoler's hands with the other things which will be sent to you that I shall mention before I have done this is the account of what I send to you one workbag two balls of worsted and one cotton and a handkerchief an old pair of Stockings and a shirt and the letter I received from my beloved sister and this book with the following sums of money.

First - £1.00

2   -   50

3   -   26

4   -   17

*   £1.91*

5   -   36

*   £1.12.7*

These I suppose will be sent in a parcel to you by some means my dearly beloved wife this is the last correspondence I can have with you so you must make yourself as easy as you possibly can and I hope God will bless you and comfort you as he as me So my blessings attend you and the children and the blessings of God be with you all now and evermore adieu adieu to all forever.

Your most affectionate husband

Jeremiah Brandreth. [16]

The workbag was the one Jeremiah worked upon decorated with flowers sewn in different colours.

William Turner sent a letter to his family, his cousin Joseph 'Manchester' Turner, who was transported to Australia, helped him to write. William added his farewell at the end.

When he was brought out upon the hurdle to be taken to the scaffold many of those that marched with him were distraught and cried openly.

At the execution at least six thousand people were in attendance, along with a detachment of Enniskilen Guards, the authorities feared an attempt to free them. They were brought out separately each on a hurdle, which was dragged around the yard, then taken to the scaffold. Jeremiah was held upon it for fear he fell off, the years living as a pauper, the weeks evading capture and for a time, a diet of bread and water maybe contributed.

Once near the scaffold William Turner and Jeremiah shook hands embraced and kissed, displaying a great deal of courage ascending the steps. Those watching said Brandreth was very calm and did not seem to fear death, when the rope was placed about his neck he held tight within his hand a black silk neck scarf he had worn.

Isaac Ludlam found comfort in prayer as he had throughout. *When asked if they had anything to say Brandreth replied "God bless you all but Lord Castlereagh," some said it was. "God bless you all and Lord Castlereagh."*

William Turner protested, "It was all Oliver and the government's doing." The Chaplain stopped this immediately by standing in front of both William and Jeremiah, while Isaac remained in prayer. The executioner pulled the cap over their heads and the three exclaimed "Into thy hands, O God, I commit my spirit." [17]

When the drop was upon them the crowd fell silent. At just gone one, they cut down and beheaded Jeremiah Brandreth, to gasps of horror and hissing from the crowd who pulled back, the military who were surrounding the scaffold sabres drawn, readied themselves to charge.

After the beheading the three were put into waiting coffins and taken to St Werburgh's church on Friargate and buried, one on top of the other in a deep grave. Jeremiah still held within his hand the silken neck scarf.

They were buried at the back in the furthest corner, at least a thousand stayed to pay their respects. There is no memorial or any mention of them to this day.

They were men that marched to secure the democracy we take so for granted now. They had little chance of gaining what they desired, three paying with their lives, others having their lives destroyed in different ways.

In the months that followed The Duke of Devonshire sent his men to pull down the houses of those known to be involved. All those left could hope for, if no kin could take them in was that the workhouse would.

*

On a visit to the area months after the event, the sixth Duke was said to be pleased with the welcome he received. Lockett the solicitor who dealt with the trial, also the Duke of Devonshire's

Land Agent, commented *'that a few heads on pikes inspired a better attitude.'* [15]

*

Those thought to be involved found it hard to gain employment again many turning them away.

The village of Pentrich lost a great many inhabitants, families fled the area in the search for work; some changing their names in an effort to rebuild their lives. Others having turned evidence considered moving prudent.

In the following years William Turner's brother Joseph moved to Sutton-in-Ashfield, and became Landlord of The Royal Foresters on Union St. the town was still a hotbed of political reform.

The government hoped after this trap was sprung no one would have the courage to fight back. We have to be thankful in the years that followed many were willing to oppose them.

*

Ann Brandreth remained at her parents' house, giving birth to Mary, in February. Eventually remarrying fifteen years later, to Henry Taylor, a Framework Knitter, moving to Mansfield.

Some years later Timothy and his family, along with his sister Mary and her family, left England for a new life in America.

Elizabeth 'Lizzie' Brandreth died of cancer at the aged of 26.

*

195

Lockett the Crown solicitor, who did so much to ensure a guilty verdict, ironically lies buried in the very same churchyard, no doubt memorialised.

*

One man and those he led set out with hope and courage until the final act was played. Jeremiah Brandreth stood fast and never once did he betray any that stood with him then, or those that did in Luddite days, even to the scaffold. Martyring himself in the hope those he led may be spared their lives.

*

Perhaps Elizabeth I, had more foresight than most, hundreds of years before, when she refused the Royal warrant to a machine that would put so many of her subjects out of work.

REFERENCE

1] W. B. Gurney.   Transcripts of the Trials. P. 162.

2] HO letter 27th June 1815 / Roger Tanner: Nottingham &
                   Pentrich Rising P.49.

3] W.B. Gurney.   The Transcripts of the Trials. P. 48.

4] W.B. Gurney.   The Transcripts of the Trials. P. 46.

5] J. Stevens.   England's Last Revolution P. 71.

6] J. Stevens.   England's Last Revolution. P. 82.

7] J. Stevens.   England's Last Revolution. P. 86.

8] W. J. Gurney. The Transcripts of the Trials. P. 58.

9]   J. Neal.   Pentrich Revolution. P.115.

10] J. Stevens.   England's Last Revolution P. 84.

11] J. Stevens. England's Last Revolution Ann's. letter.   P.99.

12 J. Stevens.   England's Last Revolution P.92.

13] W.B. Gurney. The Transcripts of The Trials. P.148.

14] W. B. Gurney. The Transcripts of the Trials. P.148.

15] R. A. Gaunt [ed] M.Parkin. 'William Jeffery Locket & the
                Pentrich Trials.' From Pentrich to Peterloo. P.87.

16] J. Stevens.   England's Last Revolution. Jeremiah's letter. P.98.

17] W. B. Gurney. The Transcripts of The Trials, execution
                speeches. P.153.

Other books and information on the Pentrich Revolution are
available from.

www.pentrichrevolution.org

Printed in Great Britain
by Amazon